close to famous

JOAN BAUER

close to famous

SCHOLASTIC INC.
New York Toronto London Auckland
Sydney Mexico City New Delhi Hong Kong

ISBN 978-0-545-43344-0

12 11 10 9 8 7 6 5 4 3 2   13 14 15 16 17/0

Printed in the U.S.A.   40

This edition first printing, January 2012

Set in Fairfield light
Book design by Nancy Brennan

In memory of Marjorie Good, my mother and best teacher.
August 28, 1925 – January 2, 2010

WITH SPECIAL THANKS TO:

Sue Grisko, who walked me through the world of challenged readers and showed me the heart of a teacher who will not give up on a child.

Steve Layne, who offered wonderful, creative solutions and outlined a character that made all the difference.

Mickey Nelson, who helped me understand a singer's mind, heart, and soul.

Catrina Ganey, who showed me an actor's strengths and struggles, and all the power Miss Charleena had inside.

Jon Foley, who guided me across West Virginia.

Jean Bauer, my daughter, who marched into the mine and found the diamonds.

Evan Bauer, my husband, who cooked for me and read endless drafts and ate cupcake after test cupcake and never complained, even when that one batch was dry.

Regina Hayes, my editor, who made this work a joy.

George Nicholson, my agent, who keeps going the extra mile.

And the midwives, JoAnn, Rita, Laura, Karen, Chris, Kally, and Donna, who told me to push, and I did.

One

THE LAST PLACE I thought I'd be when this day began is where I am, which is in a car. Mama's car to be exact, and she's driving headstrong through downtown Memphis with an Elvis impersonator on our tail. I know the Elvis; his name is Huck. He's spitting mad, honking that horn of his that you couldn't soon forget. I was there when Huck wired his old yellow Cadillac to make the horn honk out Elvis's big hit "Jailhouse Rock." Drivers pull to the side of the road when he blasts that thing. We aren't pulling over for anything.

It's eleven thirty at night, not many cars around. It rained all day; the air feels thick. Mama leans over the wheel and tries to clear off the windshield.

"Can you see?" I ask.

"Sort of."

Sort of is better than no, but not by much.

I look in the backseat at the box filled with all my cooking supplies. Big trash bags of our stuff are piled around it. We'd left fast.

"Where are we going, Mama?"

She touches her eye. It looks swollen. "We're going somewhere."

I'm hoping for a place you can find on a map.

"Try not to think about the last few hours until we have some time away from it, Foster."

How am I supposed to do that?

Memories of Huck breaking our living room window fly at me like bits of glass.

I try to fix a picture of Memphis in my mind so I can say good-bye, but mostly I think about things I'd just as soon forget, like Johnny Joe Badger, who told me I was the stupidest girl in sixth grade; like Mrs. Ritter, my main teacher, who agreed with him; like Mr. Clement Purvis, our landlord, who took singing lessons from Mama and had a voice like an injured dog, but he paid on time, so you dealt with it.

But there was Graceland, too, where the real Elvis lived. It's an actual mansion, which makes sense, because people called Elvis Presley the King of Rock and Roll. It has fountains and gardens and flowers everywhere.

Huck took me there once and walked around like he owned the place. The problem with Huck is he really thinks he's Elvis, but that's not why he's chasing us.

I grab a chocolate chip muffin from my Bake and Take carrier and take a bite. It's chewy from the touch of corn flour I used. I learned to make muffins from Marietta Morningstar, the muffin queen of Memphis. Mama says you can't just wait for things to happen, you've got to get out there and make your own breaks. So I showed up at Marietta's shop.

"I'm going to have my own restaurant someday," I told her, "and I was wondering if I could help you in your kitchen. I'll do anything at all and you don't have to pay me. I just want to learn."

She looked at me kind of strange, which I was expecting. I said, "I'll thank you in my cookbook when it comes out, and I promise I won't steal even one of your recipes."

"And who might you be, young lady?"

"I'm Foster McFee, ma'am. I got an Easy-Bake oven when I was four and the rest is history." She was paying attention now. "In case you're wondering, my mother knows I'm here. She's pretty bad in the kitchen and the worst baker ever. I'm looking for cooking role models."

Marietta Morningstar studied me like I was a recipe.

"You know more about muffins than any person in the world, probably, but I figure you had to start somewhere."

She smiled. "I walked up and down the streets of Memphis passing out free samples. People wanted more."

I reached into my bag and pulled out a pumpkin spice muffin with walnuts that was as moist as anything. "It can be plain for breakfast or I can top it with cream cheese frosting. I like a muffin that can go from day to evening."

I gave it to her. She sniffed it, nodded, and held it up.

"How do I know you're not trying to poison me?"

I wasn't expecting that question. "Ms. Morningstar, I swear, if I was going to poison you, I wouldn't ruin a perfectly fine muffin to do it."

She laughed, took a bite, and closed her eyes. "Mmmmmmmmmm." That's the sound a baker wants to hear. "Let's see. You've got canned pumpkin in here, cinnamon, ginger, nutmeg, butter, golden raisins. What else?"

How did she know the pumpkin was canned? "Vanilla," I told her. "I've been adding a touch more vanilla lately."

She stood there thinking. "I suppose we could give this a try."

I put on the apron I'd brought along. Mama made it for me. It's green with a shooting star on it. "I'm going to be the best helper you ever dreamed of!"

I helped her Tuesdays and Saturdays for almost a year before she retired and closed up shop. I measured flour, lugged around huge cartons of eggs and only dropped a few. I learned not to overmix the batter. I learned that when you run out of buttermilk, you can use milk and vinegar. I learned to make maple butter, which all by itself can make the world a better place. But mostly I learned Marietta Morningstar's main muffin truth: "Never take a fine muffin for granted," she told me. "It can open doors to the deepest recesses of the human heart."

The only recess I knew about was the kind that took place on the playground, but I sure wanted to touch hearts.

Mama turns onto the freeway. I think she could

drive us to the ends of the earth without a bathroom stop. It has been a while since I heard Huck's horn.

"You think he turned back?" I ask.

"Maybe."

She looks like she could use a hug, but it's a bad idea to hug someone who's driving. I hand her a muffin instead.

"How's your eye, Mama?" It sure looks swollen.

"A muffin will help." She takes a big bite. "*Mmmmmmmm!* I needed this."

COOK'S TIP: *Bake every day. If you have to leave town fast, you'll always have something good to eat in the car.*

Two

IT'S A LONG trip to somewhere. I went to the bathroom in Nashville and Lexington. Mama isn't talking much, and there doesn't seem to be anything left for me to think about except what happened back in Memphis.

I was in my room when I heard the noise. I thought it might be Mr. Purvis coming in the back door of our apartment building, but it wasn't him. It was Huck, who had recently become Mama's ex-boyfriend. Huck wasn't happy about that, so he broke our window.

I jumped out of bed at the sound of breaking glass and heard Mama shouting. I ran into the living room, where she slept on the couch. Huck was shaking her by the shoulders.

"Nobody leaves the King—you understand that?"

"Stop it!" I screamed. "Stop it!"

"Who's gonna sing backup for me now? Huh?" he was

shouting. *"You think you can just walk away?"*

That's when he hauled off and punched her in the eye. I did a flying leap toward him; he pushed me away.

"You keep quiet," Huck warned. But Mama always told me if anyone's trying to hurt you and they tell you to keep quiet, scream with everything you've got. I let loose the biggest scream my skinny body had. It was loud enough to wake the neighbors, who turned on their lights and started shouting.

"We're not done yet," Huck snarled. *"We're never gonna be done!"* He jumped out the window, ran to his yellow Cadillac, and sped off.

"We're out of here," Mama said, and right then that was fine by me. We packed up fast—threw toothbrushes, wet towels, clothes, food, everything we could grab into plastic bags, and loaded up our Chevy. It was like being on a reality show. *How much can you pack before the bad Elvis comes back to get you?*

Mama drove us away from Memphis.

I've been in this car ever since. I feel a tightness on my chest. I feel sweaty. When Huck was onstage sweating like Elvis, Mama would hand him scarves to put around his neck. He'd throw them out to the audience. I couldn't imagine why anyone would be interested in Huck's neck sweat, but he got his share of screaming women reaching for those things.

I roll down the car window.

"You okay, Foster?"

I'm not sure how to answer that. I just want to go someplace where there aren't any Elvises.

Mama pulls into another gas station. "You need to go?"

I head inside the snack shop. Nobody is paying attention to me, a skinny girl with long, crazy hair pulled back in a ponytail. A man is getting a slushie, a woman is buying Tootsie Rolls, a guy behind the counter shakes a key at me. "Need this?"

I head over and get the bathroom key.

"How's the weather?" he asks.

Mister, I feel like I've been hit by a tornado. "Weather's fine," I tell him.

I walk to the bathroom, hearing the *slap slap* of my flowered flip-flops on the floor. Sonny Kroll, my favorite Food Network cook, who can make a meal out of anything that's lying around, always says, "Go with what you've got." Well, I have Mama and she has me. I hope Huck has four flat tires and is left in a ditch.

I unlock the door. I wish my daddy was here. I wish that every day of my life. He was in the army. He told me soldiers were always focusing on two big moves—fighting, or leaving a place without too many casualties. I'm glad to be leaving my school in Memphis, because I felt like I was in a war in that place.

If Daddy hadn't died in the army, there would have been no Huck, Mama would probably be a big singer by now, and I'd be on my way to being the first kid cook on the Food Network, touching hearts one baked good at a time.

I look at myself in the smudged, scratched mirror. Mama says I'm distinctive looking. I've got long, thick, curly, crazy hair and a hugely wide smile. My green eyes sparkle when I cook, and I'm told I've got a memorable personality, which is what they want on TV.

I've got a dream as big as they come.

But it's hard to dream big in a dirty bathroom.

★ ★ ★

Mama is humming a song she wrote, "Go to Sleep, Little Girl." She'd sing that to me when I was little. Sometimes a song can get into your heart like nothing else. Mama's been stuck as a backup singer most of her life, but with all her talent she's really a headliner. She learned how to sing quieter than was her nature, learned how to go "Shoo wop, shoo wop" behind the headline singer. Mama knows all the moves.

Mr. Mackey, my fifth-grade teacher, had Mama come in and teach my class how to sing backup. I was so proud. Even Johnny Joe Badger got out of my face when Mama showed up. It was my second-best moment in education. The best was when Mr. Mackey asked each of us kids if we knew if any of our family had ever lived in other countries or had unusual lives. I raised my hand and said that my grandpa McFee came from Ireland, and Mama's family had roots in Africa, Russia, Sweden, Germany, and the Dominican Republic. Mr. Mackey put pushpins in a big world map for all my countries and said, "No wonder you get along with so many kinds of people, Foster. Look at all this heritage that's part of you. That's something to be proud of."

Mama drove and I fell asleep. I woke up when morning broke out around us. Now we are on a road heading toward green hills. Thick fog hangs down.

Mama peers through the window. "What's that sign say, Foster?" Then she shakes her head. "I'm sorry, Baby. I didn't mean . . ."

I bite my lip as we get closer to the sign.

Mama smiles. "I can see it now. Welcome to West Virginia."

I look out the window at the green hills. The road climbs higher. Mama takes some turns and drives higher still, round and round. Then the fog rolls in and covers the car like marshmallow cream.

"Dear God," Mama says. "Help me see."

Dear God, I pray. *Help her.*

"I've got to pull over."

That doesn't seem like a good idea, but neither does driving. She stops the Chevy and stretches out her neck. "I'm so tired."

I try to wipe the windshield, but that doesn't help. The fog is too thick to see through. I can see Mama's sweet face and her eyes closing.

"Mama!"

"I'm fine." Her eyes shut again.

I don't know where we are. I don't know where we're going. I don't know if we could be hit by another car that can't see us.

I feel the tightness come on my chest again, but I sit up straight and say out loud, "We're right where we're supposed to be."

Mama taught me to say that when I get scared. Sometimes it helps. It would be better if I could see out the window.

"We're right where we're supposed to be," I say again.

I hope that God can see us through the fog. Because if he can't, we're in big trouble.

Three

I HEARD A rumble and a roar and sat up fast. Had I been sleeping?

"What in the world . . ." Mama said.

The sun beamed through the windows of the Chevy. A wide-faced woman smiled and waved at us.

"You are two lucky ladies. Another inch and you'da been, well . . ." She shook her head and pointed down.

I looked out my side of the car. The Chevy had stopped as close to the side of a cliff as a car could without tumbling off.

Mama grabbed my hand. "We're not going to panic!"

I am!

The wide-faced woman said, "Don't worry. You're in the hands of Gotcha Towing." She was standing by a tow truck, wearing a red shirt with white lettering that I couldn't make out. "We're going to nudge up to your car a little bit and yank you out of there. Put her in neutral nice and easy." She slapped the side of the tow truck. "All right, Lester, do your magic."

I held my breath.

The tow truck backed up slowly. The woman attached a big chain to the front of the Chevy.

"Gotcha!" she shouted at us. "Hold on tight now."

Mama held my hand so tight I thought it might break.

And the strength of that truck moved us out of danger.

"Okay, girls, you're clear!"

Mama's hands were shaking as she pulled me across the driver's seat and out of the car.

"Somebody was watching over you," the woman said. "These mountain roads get nasty."

"Thank you kindly for what you did." Mama touched her swollen eye.

"That's what we're here for. I'm Kitty. That handsome thing in the truck is my Lester." Kitty was looking at Mama's bad eye. "That's a decent bruise you've got there."

"I'm all right."

"Where you folks headed?"

"Obviously a little too close to the edge."

Kitty laughed. "We all do that from time to time."

"Where's the closest town?" Mama asked.

"That's Culpepper. Twenty minutes due north. Lester and I live there."

I asked the big question. "You got any Elvis impersonators?"

She laughed. "Not a one."

I elbowed Mama.

"We'll head up to Culpepper," Mama said. "But first, I need to pay you."

Kitty shook her head. "No charge."

"Oh no, you saved us."

"If you need towing or you know someone who does, you call us." She gave her a card.

Mama asked her if she knew of a cheap place to stay.

"There's a motel down from the prison."

Prison? I elbowed Mama again.

"Not too cheap, though," Lester said from the truck.

Maybe we should talk more about this prison.

"The motel's on Route One just past the Arby's and Pizza Hut. We never had those places till that spanking new prison came to town."

"Pizza Hut's got Wednesday specials," Lester said. "'Course, it's Thursday."

"Hold on a minute." Kitty walked to Lester and they

started talking in a whisper. Then she came back. "Don't mean to pry, but in case you folks are trying to get back on your feet, we've got a—"

Mama held up a proud hand. "We're fine."

No we're not.

Kitty seemed like she was going to say something else, but she didn't. She just tipped her baseball hat, walked to the tow truck, and jumped in. Lester waved friendly. "Watch out for potholes. They're big and ugly around here."

"Wait a minute!" I ran to the Chevy, got the Bake and Take, and raced to the tow truck. "I made these myself. They're chocolate chip. Thank you for helping us."

Kitty grabbed a muffin and took a bite. "Oh, honey. My, oh my, this is good."

I handed the last muffin to Lester, who gobbled it in two bites. He wiped crumbs from his mouth. "Best thank-you I've had in a long time."

The big truck roared off down the road. I looked at the green valley below the hills. Yesterday I was making muffins; today I almost drove off a cliff.

Mama walked over and put her hand on my shoulder. "I'm sorry we had to leave the way we did, Baby. How are you doing?"

"I'm not sure."

Mama looked out at the peaceful valley. "All I could think about was getting out of there fast and making sure we were safe. I hope I did the right thing."

Me too.

★ ★ ★

The long, low gray building seemed to go on forever. It had a huge gate and a fence with curling razor wires.

"That's the prison," Mama explained.

I'd never seen a prison before, unless you count sixth grade. Most of the cars on the road were turning in to the gate.

Mama said, "Those people work there, I imagine."

"I can't imagine working at a jail."

"Better than being *in* jail."

I knew this boy, Tucker, back in Memphis. His daddy was in prison. I went to his house once—it seemed like Tucker and his mama were doing jail time, too. There was a calendar in the kitchen, and they crossed off the days until his daddy got released.

"He didn't do it," Tucker told me. "He's innocent."

I was glad when the big fence with the curled wire stopped and I didn't have to look at it anymore. I said a prayer for Tucker's daddy as a dirty truck rumbled past.

"That's a coal truck," Mama explained. "Lots of coal in West Virginia."

We drove by Arby's and Pizza Hut, and saw the motel. Mama pulled into the motel parking lot and went inside to check the rates. She came back a minute later shaking her head. "We'll find a better place."

Driving through Culpepper didn't take long. I think the jail is bigger than the town. There was a broken-down factory that looked deserted, and then a gas station.

"There's Fish Hardware," Mama said. She drove past what looked like a little restaurant. I couldn't make out the sign, which was typical for me. She pointed. "That's Angry Wayne's Bar and Grill."

Angry Wayne's?

Two red-headed boys ran around an empty lot chasing something, laughing hard. Another boy, about my age, ran down the street. He was fast. He jumped over a low fence, then another one.

Mama was smiling. "My grandpa lived in a little town like this. It feels kind of sweet."

"Angry Wayne doesn't sound sweet."

"It takes all kinds to make a town."

Down the road was a small church, boarded up. It had a big sign in front of it. I could pick out some of those words.

Church of God FOR SALE

"Church of God for sale." Mama shook her head. "Well, I never."

Mama sang at lots of churches in Memphis and Nashville, but none of them were for sale. Precious Lord was my favorite, because they had the best glazed doughnut holes during fellowship hour. Last Days Baptist had the best bathrooms, and I Am the Way Evangelical had the softest seats, but their candles didn't always stay lit. So there Mama would be, singing about the light coming into the world, and the candles would peter out.

Culpepper didn't look like a place that needed a singer or a kid who cooked her heart out and was dying to get discovered.

A woman was planting flowers in front of the church and watering them from a can. She put her hands on her hips, glared at the Church of God FOR SALE sign, and walked away like she was looking for a fight.

Mama pulled into the gas station and went inside.

That's when I saw Kitty standing by the Gotcha Towing truck, drinking a supersize bottle of pop.

I ran over. "Hi."

"Well, hi there. What have you been up to?"

"Driving. We went by the prison."

"You should see that thing at night. It gives off an unearthly glow." She made a face. "It's changed our night sky, I'll tell you that."

"Change is part a life," Lester said from the truck.

"Where are you and your mama from?"

"Memphis, and before that Nashville."

"You move around a lot?"

I kicked a stone. "Only since my daddy died."

"Sorry you've got that load."

I told how he was in the army and his helicopter got shot down. "I've got a pillowcase from Las Vegas with his things in it."

"That's good to have. My Lester was in the army."

Lester got out of the truck. He was bigger standing than he looked behind the wheel. His legs and arms were long; he had a beak nose like a bird. "Where was your daddy stationed?"

"Iraq."

Lester nodded. "Tough combat."

"Yessir."

Mama walked up, and Lester said to her, "Ma'am, we've got a mobile home behind our place. It's got two beds. You and the child here could use it. No charge."

I wasn't exactly a child, but a bed sounded good and I was sick of being in the car.

Mama looked down. "We couldn't . . ."

"It's got heat, water, and electric. Kitty and I can't bear to part with it. It might be smaller than you're used to, though."

"We only stay in small places," I mentioned.

Mama shook her head. "That's awful kind, Lester, but—"

"I'm army, too. Sergeant first class." He stood a little taller. "So you let us help you now." Lester walked back to the truck, got in, and added, "We'd better get somebody to look at that eye."

Four

"WHO DID THIS to you?" The nurse at the health clinic put an ice pack on Mama's black-and-blue eye and gave her some yellow pills.

"Doesn't matter," Mama said.

"I'd say it matters."

I figured if I told about Huck, I'd get in trouble. Mama wasn't usually like this. She was a fighter.

The nurse took the ice pack off. "We've got laws about this in West Virginia."

"Didn't happen in West Virginia," Mama mumbled.

"I need to take a photograph of your eye, Mrs. McFee."

"No. I'll just be on my—"

"That's how we do it here." The nurse got a camera out of her desk.

"You probably don't want me smiling."

The nurse clicked off a shot and put a bandage on the cut part around Mama's eye. "There's a social worker here if you need to—"

Mama shook her head. "We'll be on our way."

"If you change your mind . . ."

Mama shook her head again.

"You come back in ten days, Mrs. McFee, and I'll check it."

Mama put on her mega-star sunglasses and we headed out of the clinic. "All right. That's over."

It didn't feel over to me. We walked to the Chevy. "Do you think Huck might hurt other women, Mama?"

She stopped.

I looked at her. "I think he might."

She unlocked the door. "There are things, Foster, you don't understand."

I understood that the least little thing could set him off.

Foster, you stop looking at me like that!

Like what, Huck?

Like I don't know, but you stop it!

Foster, it's ten o'clock and you're still awake!

Well, maybe if you'd stop yelling . . .

You'll hear a lot more than that, girl, if you don't go to sleep.

Once he started screaming at me and calling me a loser because I got a bad report card. I told Mama, and that's when she told him they were through. He tried to sweet-talk his way back into her heart. He wrote her a song and brought chocolate and gave me an Elvis doll that twisted at the hips. But Mama said, *adiós, sayonara, get lost.*

The next day he broke our window. I guess if I'd kept my mouth shut, we'd still be in Memphis. But if I'd done that, I'd be agreeing with Huck. I'm trying hard not to agree with anybody who says I'm a loser.

* * *

The trailer was silver, and the top half was round like a bullet with little windows in front and back. It looked like an old-fashioned spaceship had landed in the yard.

"This here's our Airstream," Kitty said. "Lester's pride and joy. Next to me, of course." She batted her eyes.

From the porch, Lester shouted, "She's an International twenty-five footer with a new floor, wheel covers, battery, storage tank, hydraulic disk brakes, new fridge, oven cooktop, new converter charger, new window seals, new hot water heater. I did her up myself."

I'd never seen anything like this. It sat behind their old house right next to a tomato garden.

"Come August," Kitty said, "we'll be up to our earlobes in tomatoes."

It was June. I love tomatoes, but no way would we be here in August.

"We call this old girl the Silver Bullet." Kitty opened the door. "Oh, the memories that bless and burn."

It was hot inside and a little dusty, but it felt magical. There was a tiny kitchen with dishes in a see-through cupboard. A green couch wrapped around the wall, and there was a low bookcase, a hooked rug, and pictures of a man and woman hiking, fishing, and hugging on a beach.

"That's me and Lester in younger days. We crossed America twice in this beauty."

The bed was at the end next to a little closet. It had a yellow-and-green striped cover. Kitty opened a door to a small bathroom with a shower. I poked my head in. Every inch of space was used. Back in the main room, Kitty grabbed a handle on the wall. "Watch this." She pulled, and down came another bed.

"Cool," I said.

Kitty pounded the mattress. "It's seen better days."

I flopped on the bed. "This is wonderful!"

"What a place this is." Mama got out her wallet. "I want to pay you rent and—"

Kitty shook her head. "We're not using it, and we can't bear to get rid of it. Lester's daddy lived in it for eight years. Man was sharp as a tack until the day he died. He keeled over in the kitchen one day and that was it. We keep it as a kind of memorial to him. You just settle in."

I wished she hadn't mentioned the part about him dying in the kitchen.

"I insist." Mama tried to press money into Kitty's hand.

But Kitty wouldn't take it. "There was a time when me and Lester were flat-out broke and some folks gave us the room above their garage until we got back on our feet. I'm just passing that on."

I want to be like that someday.

There was a stuffed fish hanging above the sink. "Lester's daddy was a fisherman," Kitty explained. "He said you could never catch the smart fish, they were the ones that got away. That was the biggest bass he ever caught. We had it mounted for him on his eighty-fifth birthday. He'd talk to it day and night."

I thought she said he was sharp as a tack. I looked at the fish and figured if it got caught, that meant it was stupid. It might take some time to get used to cooking with a stupid, dead fish looking on.

Mama said, "I don't know what to say."

I did. "Thank you!" I gave Kitty a big hug, went outside to the Chevy, and started unloading. A black cat with a white face meowed at my feet.

"Hey, cat."

I carried two big trash bags into the house. I went back for my box of cooking stuff. The cat was purring near my leg.

"He doesn't come around to just anyone," Kitty said. "He must sense you're good. Elvis, this here is Foster."

Elvis? My heart beat fast as the cat looked at me.

"If you say 'Hi, Elvis' back you'll have sealed the relationship."

I gulped. "Hi, Elvis." Huck used to make me call him Elvis when Mama wasn't around. Elvis the cat twitched his whiskers and crept away.

Is there any place on this earth without an Elvis?

Five

WE STARTED UNPACKING. We didn't have much, but getting it put away gave me a hopeful feeling. Mama and me try not to let belongings be too important. The number one thing I've got isn't pots and pans, it's Daddy's Las Vegas pillowcase with all his things inside. I was looking around the Airstream thinking where I would put it. Not near the fish.

Mama looked around, too. "I can drape a pretty sheet near the bed and you can pull it down when you're sleeping. We can do this place up just like home."

I was going through the big box where I had put Daddy's pillowcase. I took out my robe, a blanket, and my shooting-star apron. The pillowcase wasn't there. We left so fast, maybe I had shoved it somewhere else. I headed back out to the Chevy. Elvis the cat wanted my attention.

"I don't have time for anything named Elvis. You shoo."

The back of the Chevy was empty; I looked through the trunk. I looked through the trunk again, and this time I was close to crying, because I couldn't find Daddy's pillowcase anywhere.

"Mama!"

She ran out.

"You've got the pillowcase, right?"

One look at her face said she didn't. We searched the car again. We searched everything in the trailer *again*.

It wasn't there!

My most prized possession, with Daddy's dog tags from the army and his papers and the special award he got for getting killed and the letters he sent me and his cuff links from when he and Mama got married and his little flag of Ireland and his donkey key ring that you press and get a *hee-haw* sound.

"You said we had everything!" I shouted.

"I . . . I thought we did."

"You should have checked!"

"*Baby, I'm sorry.*"

She reached out to me, but I pulled away. Elvis the cat came up, meowing.

"Shut up!" I screamed. "Don't come back!" The stupid cat ran off.

I tucked my knees to my chest and cried like Daddy had died again.

* * *

I was in the car with Mama; we were driving into town to pick up some food. My eyes had stopped crying, but my heart hadn't.

"I know you miss your daddy."

I looked out the window. We'd kept our old answering machine with his voice saying, "You've reached Kevin, Rayka, and Foster. We're out doing something fun, so leave a number and we'll call you back." I had played that over and over until it broke. Now I can't remember the sound of his voice. I used to sleep in his army shirt. I took excellent care of it. I'd wash it good and hang it outside to dry, until a skunk came along and used it for target practice. Everything I had that he'd touched got taken.

Mama drove by the Church of God FOR SALE. I couldn't imagine why anyone would want to buy that place. She turned into the lot for a little grocery. The sign out front had one easy word: FOOD.

This place didn't look like much.

Mama adjusted her sunglasses. "This should be an adventure."

I'd had enough adventures for one day. We got out of the Chevy and walked inside.

"It ain't over till it's over." A tall woman said that to the man behind the counter.

"That's for sure, Percy," the man said.

"We're not giving up without a fight."

"You're a fighter, Percy." The man nodded to us.

"Mr. Frank Fish hasn't seen anything yet!"

The man smiled. "I think he knows that."

"Church of God for sale," she snarled. "It's a disgrace." She walked out the door, and then I remembered. She was the lady I'd seen planting flowers outside the church.

"You ladies finding what you need?" the man asked, friendly.

"We are, thank you kindly."

It was good I came along, because Mama would buy Hamburger Helper and canned chili if I wasn't there to watch her. I had started cooking partly out of self-defense. I found some cheese, a ham steak, ground beef, eggs, milk, butter, chocolate chips, juice, canned tomatoes, pasta, and instant butterscotch pudding, the secret ingredient for my soon-to-be-famous butterscotch muffins.

We headed to the counter.

"New to town?" the man asked.

I checked my watch. "We've been here exactly four hours."

He chuckled. "Say, that's real new." He rang up our food. "Staying awhile?"

"Awhile," Mama said.

"Welcome to Culpepper. I'm Jarvis."

"Rayka McFee," Mama said, "and this is my daughter, Foster."

Just then the door opened and Percy marched back in like she had a storm inside of her. She pointed a finger at Jarvis "And if that real estate woman comes sniffing around, you tell her she's going to have the fight of her sweet life if she tries to sell the church. You tell her that!"

Jarvis said, "Rayka and Foster, meet Perseverance Wilson, the defender of all that's right and true."

Mama grinned. "You've got a big job, Ms. Wilson."

Perseverance Wilson smiled bright. "Somebody's got to do it." Her smile took over most of her face.

I waved hi. I'd never met a defender of all that's right and true before. She sounded like a superhero. She didn't look like one. She was wearing a long orange crinkly skirt, a yellow blouse, and big hoop earrings. She was tall with short hair curled tight around her head. Her skin was darker than Mama's.

"Rayka and Foster are new to town," Jarvis said.

She looked at Mama's eye bandage. Mama was wearing her megastar sunglasses, but you could still see the gauze. "Don't get many new folks here."

I was starting to see why.

Perseverance Wilson turned to Jarvis. "You seen Fish around?"

Jarvis smiled. "I imagine he's hiding."

"When you see him, tell him I'm going to impart a depth of misery to his very soul, and I'll be singing a song of joy when I do it."

"I'd rather you told him."

Jarvis shook his head as she left. I knew Mama wouldn't say a peep about this, but me, I have trouble keeping quiet.

"She seems upset," I began.

"You don't know the half of it."

Right then a short boy came running into the store

waving a sheet of blue paper. "I got Miss Charleena's list and she's low this time; lower than yesterday, even!"

I looked at Mama.

Jarvis read the list, lifted a bag of coffee off the shelf behind him, and put it in a box with a big bottle of mouthwash.

"I'll get the syrup and the frozen waffles," the boy said and headed down the aisle.

Jarvis called after him. "That special honey she wanted from New Zealand hasn't come in yet."

The boy turned around. He looked worried.

"I've got another blow for you, Macon. We're out of Ho Hos and Ding Dongs."

"Miss Charleena's not going to like that!"

"She's going to have to deal with the disappointment until the Hostess truck comes."

I grabbed Mama's arm.

What kind of place is this?

Six

MAMA PULLED OUT of the FOOD lot as a gray bus with black letters went by. The men inside it didn't look friendly.

"That's the prison bus, Foster."

I got a creepy feeling. "Those men are headed to jail?"

"The sign said Culpepper Penitentiary."

It should have said, CRIME DOESN'T PAY. I watched the bus disappear around the corner.

Mama drove down a bumpy street trying to miss the potholes. Little houses and a few trailers were set back from the road. We drove by a closed-up factory with a faded sign.

"Colonel Culpepper's Jams and Jellies," Mama read. "No Trespassing."

Mama reads to me a lot. My brain closes up when I open a book. I almost flunked sixth grade because of it. My second-grade teacher told Mama I would grow out of it, but it feels more like it's grown all over me.

Mama turned the Chevy down the dirt road, past the broken fence, around to the back of Kitty and Lester's place, and parked by the Silver Bullet that was gleaming in the late-day light.

The tow truck was gone. Kitty and Lester were probably off rescuing somebody. In front of the door to the Bullet were two outdoor chairs—one green and one blue—and a little table. Those hadn't been there before. Mama smiled at the chairs and opened the door. I carried the groceries inside.

Lester's daddy's stupid, dead fish seemed to be looking at me. "I'm baaaaaack," I said to it. I put the food away, thinking about the pillowcase. Did I drop it outside the car? Did it get run over? Did Mr. Purvis throw it out when he got the note that we'd left?

"I'm thinking I need to call Mr. Purvis, Foster."

"I'm thinking you need to right now!"

She took out her phone and shooed me outside.

I sat in the blue chair and felt the wind blow gently

all around me. Mr. Purvis didn't like kids much, but I had wowed him with my brown sugar brownies.

I hoped he remembered those brownies. Of course, they were hard to forget.

Elvis the cat was watching me. He meowed and I meowed back. He didn't like that.

"It's nothing personal," I told him. "If your name was Fluffy or Princess I'd like you fine." Elvis licked his paw.

Mama came out and lowered herself into the green chair like she was carrying a heavy load. "He doesn't have it."

"He's lying!"

Mama crossed her arms. "Why do you say that?"

"Because he's mad at us for leaving like that! He's got it, I know he does!"

"I don't think that's true. He was very nice to me on the phone." Mama sighed. "I don't know what else to do."

"You could call the neighbors!"

"I don't have their numbers, Foster!"

"You could call Mr. Purvis back and tell him to put up a sign in the front hall about it!"

Mama put in the call and Mr. Purvis said he'd put up a sign. She gave him her phone number.

"Okay?" she said to me.

"Okay."

She started humming a song she'd written for me last year on my birthday. It's called "Foster's Song." Having a song named after you is this side of cool. She sang it soft and low.

> *Hush now, it's going to be all right.*
> *The night is coming, but we've got the light*
> *And it's shining all around us so don't you be afraid.*
> *Don't let the problems of the day invade.*
> *Let them go away. Let them go away.*
> *And wait for the morning and the bright new day.*

I felt those words coming down on me like soft rain. She sang it again, and then I sang with her:

> *Let them go away. Let them go away.*
> *And wait for the morning and the bright new day.*

★ ★ ★

The new day wasn't too bright, it was cloudy, and when I asked Mama what would happen if we didn't find Daddy's pillowcase, she said, "Then you'll have your daddy safe in your heart, and that's a place where you can never lose any part of him."

Mama went to take a shower, and I headed for the kitchen.

Bake it big.

Bake it proud.

That's what Sonny Kroll always says on his cooking show. He'd been a marine. Eddington Carver, my best friend in Memphis, once asked me, "So how did you handle it when your dad got killed?" And I told him, "I watched Sonny Kroll's show." Eddington's box turtle Brucie had just died and he needed something to feel better, so we started watching Sonny's show together, and before long we formed the Two Kids Cooking Club. At the end of our meetings we tapped our rolling pins and said, "We're on this road together." That's how Sonny ended his show.

You really get to know somebody when you share a meal. Eddington's mama used to eat standing over the sink, but we got her sitting at the table and living right. That's what home cooking does. I'm going to talk about this when I get my show.

I got out my muffin pan and decided to practice. TV chefs have to cook, smile, *and* talk at the same time, which isn't easy. I gave Lester's daddy's stupid, dead fish my amazing TV grin.

"You know, people are cooking pretty complicated recipes today. In my opinion, you don't have to go crazy on ingredients."

I mixed flour, sugar, salt, and baking powder in a bowl. "That's why I love this butterscotch muffin. You can make it up easy as one, two, three." Easy recipes that taste great are big on cooking shows. I added the box of butterscotch pudding mix, three eggs, and milk, and stirred it up. "Don't kill the batter with overbeating, because holes can form in the muffin when it bakes." I smiled, because smiling is important on TV. It doesn't matter how you feel inside, if the cameras are on you—*grin.*

I put paper liners in the pan and winked at the dead fish. "Make sure the batter's even in each tin," I said, filling them. "And now"—I opened the oven door grinning—"pop it in the oven." I don't know why so many cooks say "pop it in the oven," but they do.

I wiped my hands and stood at the sink. "I want to tell all you kids out there who are watching me, life gets hard sometimes. Just don't give up, okay? Don't give up on your dreams. And remember, when your heart is ready to break, that's the perfect time to bake. Okay. See you next time." I waved. That's my close. I'm still working on it.

I made Mama coffee and set the little table for breakfast like it was a celebration. The table was tucked under the rounded window. It looked like a booth in a restaurant. I sat down on a yellow cushion. Part of me felt like a little girl in a grown-up playhouse, the other part felt like a doughnut that had just lost its hole.

I didn't hear the shower running anymore, but from inside the bathroom, I could hear Mama crying.

Ask any kid and they'll tell you how hard it is to hear your mother cry.

★ ★ ★

Mama loved the muffins, and I didn't once ask why she was crying. Like a multiple choice test at school where none of the answers seems very good, sometimes there isn't one right answer.

"Do you like it here?" she asked me. "The town and all."

"There's not much to it, Mama."

"I know."

"I feel kind of different." I sighed. "I guess I'd feel that wherever."

She grinned. "You are different. The best kind of different. You up for staying a couple of weeks and seeing how it feels then?"

"It's cool living in the Silver Bullet."

"And the price is right."

Mama's real careful with money. When Daddy died, the army sent us a chunk of money called "death benefits." She's got some saved for me to go to college, but I'm not sure she'll have to spend much on my education, since it took all I had to squeak through sixth grade.

"You think they have a grocery other than FOOD, Mama?"

"I don't know."

"How about a restaurant other than Angry Wayne's?"

"There's Pizza Hut and Arby's."

"I meant one that would care about dessert."

"Well now." Mama laughed. "We're getting down to serious matters."

COOK'S TIP: *Sometimes just sitting with someone you love and having a warm muffin can help set things right.*

Seven

FOOD WAS THE only grocery in town. Mama and I were there by the freezer section when the short boy I'd seen the other day ran down the middle aisle waving a piece of blue paper like it was the most important thing in West Virginia.

"Miss Charleena needs bug spray, Pepto-Bismol, and a big jar of chocolate syrup," he shouted at Jarvis. "And she needs to order more of the . . ." He looked at his list. ". . . green tea eye-lift pads with mung bean concentrate."

"Think that'd make you go blind," Jarvis said.

I walked to the fruit and vegetable section. I needed carrots and zucchini for a muffin I learned to make from Marietta Morningstar. There was only one bag of carrots left. I reached for it.

"You can't have that!"

I looked up. The short boy was standing there, desperate. "Miss Charleena has carrots on her list, and I can't go back without them."

I could have said, "I was here first," but Mama taught me to be reasonable around unreasonable people.

"Here," I said. "Take them."

He took them and looked at me. "Thank you."

I shrugged.

"Thank you on behalf of Miss Charleena."

I didn't say you're welcome.

"You're new," he said.

"Yeah."

"You probably don't know about Miss Charleena."

I never wanted to meet her. I knew that much.

He lowered his voice. "She's Culpepper's most famous person and I work for her. When she needs things, she needs them right away."

I looked around for Mama, but I didn't see her. "Well, you've got the carrots."

He turned the bag over in his hands. "I will tell Miss Charleena of your kindness."

"It's no big deal." But I was curious. "How famous is she?"

"She was a movie and TV actress. She's won an

Emmy, a Golden Globe, and was nominated for two Oscars."

Wow.

"Miss Charleena should have won those Oscars, too. Between you and me, she was robbed. She played an alcoholic wife of a murderer in *The Deepest Part of the Ocean* and a desperate immigrant mother in *My Name Is Tess*."

"I never heard of those." I like movies that make me laugh, like *Uncle Raymond's Bad Vacation*.

He cocked his head and looked at me. I picked out a few tomatoes and some bananas. I hate being stared at.

"I make documentary films," he said.

I'm not sure what a documentary film is, but I'm close to positive they don't get made by this boy.

"You have a very interesting face," he added. "And you would look good on film. Has anyone told you that?"

"No." I smoothed back my hair. I've thought about having a cooking DVD to go with my TV show and hugely popular restaurant. I walked to the checkout, where Jarvis was putting bug spray, Pepto-Bismol, and chocolate syrup into a bag.

The boy grabbed three rolls of toilet paper and

followed me. "I'm Macon Dillard, Miss Charleena's assistant."

"I'm Foster."

He nodded his head. "Foster is a very interesting name. I bet there's a story behind your name."

It was Mama's maiden name. There's a big story about my middle name, but I'm keeping that to myself.

"Miss Charleena didn't have to change her name when she went to Hollywood. Some actors do." He pushed past me. "Is it okay if I go first? Miss Charleena gets nervous if I don't come back right away."

I stepped aside as Macon checked the bill, signed his name, took the grocery bag, and said, "We'll talk again, Foster." He dashed out the door.

Jarvis rang up my order. "The lady he works for, Charleena Hendley, is our local entertainment."

"*The* Charleena Hendley?" It was Mama.

"The one and only," Jarvis said.

"A famous actress lives here instead of Hollywood?" I couldn't quite believe it.

"She lives here, but she brought some of Hollywood with her."

★ ★ ★

"How can you not know Charleena Hendley?" Mama asked me.

I shrugged. There are lots of holes in my education.

"I love her movies. I read she left acting and moved back home after her rotten husband dumped her for that supermodel, Bliss. I didn't know home was *here*." Mama drove past the shut-down factory. "What that woman's got inside is amazing."

That was some compliment coming from Mama, who had more inside than most people dreamed about. It was in her like special cream filling.

Once, back in Memphis, she let it all out.

She was onstage waiting for Huck. It was a rehearsal; I was the only one in the audience. It started with a mic check. Mama sang into the mic and something magical happened. She was singing so good, the piano player sat down and started following her; the bass player did, too. The drummer ran out onstage and pounded out the beat. Mama threw back her head and sang it strong and true about a woman who'd been done wrong by a man, but she was going to be all right. *Oh yeah. She was going to be all right.*

I stood up and applauded, and so did the other

musicians. I was shouting, "Encore, encore!" Mama laughed and took a bow, but then Huck marched out onstage in his tight, white Elvis outfit, shouting, "What's going on here?" They went into "Love Me Tender," a big Elvis hit. I watched Mama step back into the shadows, letting all the light beam on Huck.

But nobody forgot Mama's song.

I wish somebody could take an X-ray of my heart to show me all I've got inside.

Mama says it's more than I can imagine, which is why my middle name is Akilah. It's an African name that means "intelligent one who reasons." I've tried to tell Mama that with my grades, I don't deserve that name, but she just says, "I know what's in you, Foster Akilah McFee."

My daddy wrote that to me in a letter when he was in Iraq. Not that I could read it—Mama read it to me— but I have the part memorized where he said, *You live right, now. You work hard. Don't waste your talents. I know what you've got inside.*

I haven't asked Mama to read me any of Daddy's letters for a long time. She started crying bad the last time she did. She got as far as, "Dear Foster, today we played baseball and I got a home run. It's strange playing baseball with fighter planes zooming overhead." Mama lost it right there.

I used to take out Daddy's letters, unfold them, and let my fingers go back and forth over the lines. Daddy wasn't rich when it came to money, but he was rich in his heart. I think when it came to his heart, Daddy was an official millionaire. Mostly, when I remember him, I remember him happy.

Mama called Mr. Purvis back twice, but he said no one had seen the pillowcase.

I guess that part of Daddy is lost to me now.

Eight

I DON'T KNOW how Macon found me. I'd just washed my hair and wrapped a towel around my head, and there he was at the door wearing jeans, sneakers, and a blue T-shirt that had this across the chest:

DOCS ROCK

I went outside. He stared at me. "You look different without your hair."

"It's not like I lost it, it's under the towel." Now I felt weird with a towel wrapped around my head.

He smiled. "You like my shirt?"

"What's it mean?"

"*Docs* is short for *documentaries*. Docs rock."

Okay.

"Do you know why documentaries rock?" he asked.

"They're about issues. You can't be a documentary filmmaker unless you have issues."

"What kind of issues have you got?"

Macon looked down. "Well, the thing is, I need to find some issues. I need to push the envelope and get angry about things and turn that anger into a film." He sat on a log and looked around. This boy didn't seem too angry.

"I want to know if you want to be in my movie."

I'd never had anyone ask me this. "Do I have to have issues?"

"It would help."

"I'm not sure I've got good ones."

"What makes you angry, Foster?"

"Teachers who say you're not trying when you are. People who pretend to be good and turn out to be bad."

"I don't like those things either." Macon leaned forward like he wanted to punch something. "You know what makes me mad? When you've got a big dream and nobody takes you seriously."

"I hate that, too."

Macon took a deep breath. "Culpepper's got issues. We've got this new prison that was supposed to come in and help the town with jobs and support local businesses, but it hasn't done much of that; mostly it's made people nervous and angry. It's changed the way people feel about the town. We used to be the place where Colonel Culpepper's Jams and Jellies were made, and they were great, Foster. But now the factory is gone, so many people got laid off, and the prison didn't hire many locals. It's hard to get work here. It's hard to see things changing! That's what I want to make my movie about."

"That sounds important."

He sighed sadly. "It is. But nobody will talk to me about it."

"I'm talking to you."

"I *mean* adults." Macon stood, which didn't make much difference. "And there's another thing. I don't go telling everybody this, Foster. I haven't saved enough to buy a movie camera yet and my mom won't let me use her camera phone, so even if someone would talk to me, I couldn't film it!" He put his head in his hands.

"How do you make a movie without a camera?" I was just curious, but Macon's cheeks got red.

"*Of course, Foster, the actual movie can't be made, but there's lots to do before principal photography!*"

I started drying my hair. "Like what?"

"You don't seem very interested in this! Here I am

talking to you about my big dream and you're drying your hair!"

"It's wet!"

"I'll come back when it's dry!" Macon stormed off. Elvis the cat slithered toward me. From inside the Bullet, I heard Mama's cell phone ring.

"Foster," Mama shouted, "get that, will you?"

I ran inside and found the phone. "Hello?"

There was a pause on the other end, then I heard the low, familiar voice. "Well, little Foster, this here's your old friend *Elvis*. I got something I think you want."

Nine

I FROZE AT the sound of Huck's voice.

"Foster, now I've been trying to find you and your mama."

I didn't say a word.

"Girl, are you there?"

I held my breath so he couldn't hear my breathing. I was sure he could hear my heart pounding.

"I know you're there, sugar. You just listen to old Elvis. You listen to the King."

I heard clanging on the line.

"Know what that is?"

I pictured him swaggering around in his Elvis getup. I didn't say a word.

"Let's see if you can guess. It's a pillowcase with the words *Las Vegas* on the front, and inside—"

"That's mine!" I hollered.

He chuckled. "Let's see here—there's some kinda little flag and some letters and—"

"*You leave those alone!*"

Mama walked in. "Who are you talking to?"

"*Shhhhhhhh!*" I covered the phone.

"*Who is it?*"

"Huck," I whispered. "He's got the pillowcase."

Mama froze.

"You put your mama on the phone and we can work this out."

I wanted Daddy's pillowcase bad, but not as bad as I wanted never to see Huck again.

"Give me the phone, Baby."

I looked up at Lester's daddy's stupid, dead fish and realized it was dead because it got fooled by a worm on a hook. I'm not getting fooled.

"Give me the phone, Baby."

I backed away from her. "No ma'am."

"*Foster!*"

"Now," Huck was saying, "your mama and I can work this all out. You know us—we fight one minute and make up the next. It's no big deal."

I flipped the phone shut and said close to the

hardest thing I've ever said in my life. "I don't need the pillowcase, Mama."

The phone started ringing again.

I turned it off. Mama sat down on the couch and touched her hurt eye. "What did he say?"

"He said you could work it out."

She shook her head. "How did he get the pillowcase?"

"I didn't ask."

Mama touched the fringe on the hanging sheet. I wanted to yank a sheet around our whole lives.

"How come you didn't turn Huck in when he hit you, Mama?"

"I don't know." She sounded so tired. She walked into the bathroom and shut the door.

I walked to the kitchen.

I put on my shooting star apron, got out my baking pan, opened the refrigerator, and took out tortillas, tomato sauce, salami, and cheese.

"Today on *Cooking with Foster* we're going to make smiling pizzas for sad days." I put two tortillas down on the pan, spread red sauce over them, and sprinkled on mozzarella, garlic powder, and oregano.

"Be careful the cheese doesn't go over the edge or

it'll spill over on the pan and start smoking. That can make your whole kitchen stink. I'm going to turn the oven dial to four-fifty." I did that, smiling. "And now I'm getting my best knife"—I held it up—"and I'm slicing a thin round of salami into a smiley shape just like this. Don't make it too thick. I'm putting that on the pizza and cutting two small circles and putting them down for eyes." I looked at it. "We need eyebrows, don't you think?" I looked around, got some sliced olives, and put them over the eyes.

"All right, I'm popping this in the oven, and in about ten minutes, it's going to be great." I smiled at Lester's daddy's stupid, dead fish.

"Let me tell you something about sad days. They're just part of life, but the best thing you can do on the happy days or on the sad ones is to do what you do best with everything you've got. The bravest man I knew told me that." I leaned against the sink and crossed my arms tight. "He died in a war. I wish war had never been invented. But right now, let's have a moment of silence for every person lost in every war that has ever been, and all the kids who miss them."

I stood by the sink, hugging myself, hearing the clock *tick tock*. I'm not sure how long a moment of silence is supposed to be, but after a while, it seemed long enough.

I heard the pizzas sputtering, put on my oven mitt, took the pizzas out of the oven, and laughed at the smiley faces. "See, they're perfect. Golden and bubbly, but not burned. And you're going to love the thin, crispy crust." I leaned over to smell it. "Don't forget to smell what you've made, because that's part of the fun. I learned that from Sonny Kroll, the second bravest man I know, although I don't really know him. And don't forget to turn the oven off. That's a major kitchen safety tip."

I turned the oven off, got out my pizza wheel, and started cutting. "You can't make a smiling pizza and not feel better. We're going to talk about everything you can think of on this show."

★ ★ ★

Huck started calling a few times each day. Mama stopped answering her phone, but she still had the messages to deal with about how he loved her and he couldn't live without her.

It's funny, I hadn't minded Huck in the beginning. He was actually pretty nice. He told me, "One of these days, you're going to turn into a fine reader."

"I don't think so, Huck."

"Don't go saying that now. You think I became one

of the best Elvises overnight? No, girl. I set my mind to get there. I'd wear long underwear so I could sweat like a pig onstage. Every day, I'd ask myself, what would Elvis do?"

But when my report card came, he called me a loser. He could never make up his mind.

I think he loved Mama in his own way, but he didn't have the kind of love that wanted her to shine. Huck had room for only one star in the sky—his.

"You're not going to see him again, right?" I asked Mama.

"I'm not going to see him," she promised.

Mama started making the rounds in Culpepper to find work. She went to the prison and tried to get a job answering the phone, but they weren't hiring. Jarvis at FOOD didn't need help; neither did the gas station. Then Mama and I were in Fish Hardware buying a mop and Mama decided to go for it.

"I'm handy as all get-out," she told Mr. Fish. "I can fix a toilet, repair a car, and work a power saw." Mama learned all that from books. It just shows you how lucky good readers are. "You need some life in here," Mama added.

From the back I heard a voice say, "We sure do,

Daddy." A girl a little older than me walked up. She had freckles and straight brown hair that touched her shoulders. Mr. Fish, a gray, boring man, seemed nervous.

"You can try me out for a week," Mama said.

Mr. Fish coughed. "Well, I'm not sure."

"We've got lots of new things planned for the store," the girl announced.

"Maybe," her father told her.

"Daddy!" The girl put her hands on her hips and stared at her father as the door opened and Perseverance Wilson marched in. Mr. Fish looked like he wanted to run.

"Fish," she shouted, "we need to talk."

"I'm just getting our new employee here situated, Ms. Wilson." He looked at Mama. "When did you say you could start?"

Mama grinned. "How about now?"

"My daughter, Amy, will show you around." He walked quickly out the door.

Perseverance Wilson called after him, "You can run, Fish, but you can't hide." She turned to Amy. "Nothing personal, honey."

Amy bit her lip and walked Mama to the back, saying, "I've been reorganizing the store so things are easier to find. Over there is where we'll have our Cool Tools section. That's my idea."

"I like it," Mama said.

"My father doesn't."

Percy eyed me. "How you getting on?"

"Okay."

"You making friends?"

I shrugged.

She took me by the arm. "Come and meet Garland. He's about your age and close to the finest boy God ever put on this earth. I'm not just saying that because he's my son." We went outside, and a tall boy with short, curly hair was doing stretches. He was the one I'd seen running. Percy cleared her throat. "This here is Foster, and she needs a friend."

I wish she hadn't said it that way! "I'm new," I explained.

Garland smiled real friendly. "You run?" he asked me.

"I bake."

He thought about that. "What do you bake?"

"Just about anything."

"Chocolate cake?"

"Yeah."

"Blueberry pie?"

I nodded.

He tied his sneaker. "Snickerdoodles, oatmeal cookies . . ."

"Yes," I said. "And a hundred other things."

"How come you're not baking?"

"How come you're not running?"

Garland grinned good enough for TV. "'Cause I'm talking to you." He checked his watch. "But I've got to practice or my coach will kill me."

He sped down the street, jumping over fences. Percy watched him go. "See, it's not so bad around here."

I tried my best not to smile too big.

Ten

"I'M HERE TO talk to you about a once-in-a-lifetime opportunity."

Macon stood by our open door and took a deep breath. "I talked to Miss Charleena about you, Foster, and even though she doesn't like having people around, even though she is still grieving the loss of so much of her life and all the awful things her ex-husband did to her in public . . ." He breathed. "But at least the Hostess truck came in. We can all be grateful for *that*."

"What is it, Macon?"

He looked up at me. "She said that you can come to her house with me. I've got to work in her garden, and you can help."

"Get ready for an experience," Lester shouted from the tomato garden.

"So, Foster, do you want to come with me to meet Miss Charleena tomorrow?"

I'd never met somebody who was famous before, even though I'd never heard of her.

"I've got to ask my mama."

"Ask her what?" Mama walked up.

Macon went into his once-in-a-lifetime-opportunity speech.

"How long have you been working for her?" Mama asked him.

"Six months. Miss Charleena asked who was the most responsible kid in town, and my name kept coming up."

"Well now. That's something."

"It's perfectly safe, Mrs. McFee."

Mama walked over to Lester, who was tending his tomato patch. They talked a few minutes. Mama came back. I couldn't read her face.

"I'll say yes under one *very specific condition*."

I held my breath.

Mama grinned. "Remember *everything*—how her house looks, what she's wearing, and everything she says!"

★ ★ ★

Mama and I stayed up late talking about Miss Charleena's movies and how she was one of those actors who could disappear into any part she was playing.

"How do you think I should be around her?" I asked.

"Be yourself. Remember, she puts her pants on one leg at a time, just like you."

I was trying to remember that the next morning as Macon and I made the final chug up Marigold Hill to Miss Charleena's house.

"Some people think she's kind of into herself and doesn't care about other people," Macon explained. "This is totally wrong, Foster. She's known a lot of sorrow. Last month, she thought she was dying."

"Of what?"

"Something mysterious."

We walked up a gravel path to a huge gray house. It had a white painted porch with white furniture, and hanging plants were everywhere. Each window had white shutters, but you couldn't see inside. All the curtains were closed.

"Miss Charleena's not too happy about her view." Macon pointed to the prison below. "That's why she built that big fence."

It was the tallest fence I'd ever seen.

We walked down a stone path, past a garden with blue flowers. Next to it was another garden with yellow flowers, and across from that was a garden filled with pink roses. I could definitely live here.

"Miss Charleena doesn't like different flowers mixed up together. She likes everything a certain way. It's really important that you don't do anything wrong, Foster."

That got me nervous. "Like what?"

He took out a ring of keys and headed to the back door. "Miss Charleena doesn't like anyone tracking a mess through her house, so you've got to take off your shoes."

If I'd known that, I wouldn't have come with holes in my socks. I took my shoes off, tried to twist my socks so my toes didn't show through. Macon shook his head. "Miss Charleena won't like seeing your toes."

"Maybe she can just look up."

Macon seemed pained. We headed through a screened-in porch past fancy white furniture with pink and green pillows. It's hard to walk regular when your socks are twisted. I picked up one of the pillows. It was so soft. I thought about Daddy's pillowcase.

"Don't go touching things. Miss Charleena doesn't like that."

I put the pillow back as two little white dogs ran through a doggy door and out into the yard.

"That's Tracy and Hepburn," Macon said. "Don't pet them if your hands aren't clean. Miss Charleena doesn't like that." He whispered. "Sometimes she changes her mind about what she likes."

"Then how will I know?"

"You won't know, Foster! That's why you have to be really careful! I'm trying to give you the basics of how not to mess up."

I nodded.

He opened the back door. "Don't yell in the house, don't slam the door, and do not ever open the curtains. Miss Charleena really doesn't like that."

I groaned. "Is there anything she *does* like?"

"Well, that depends," said a low, Southern voice that gave me the shivers.

A tall, beautiful woman wearing a long white shirt, blue jeans, and dangling jewel earrings stepped forward. "So far, darlin', I'm not too impressed with you."

Eleven

"MISS CHARLEENA," MACON stammered. "Uh . . . this . . . is my friend that I talked to you about and you said it was okay to bring her here . . . and . . ."

Miss Charleena stood there looking at me. She had blonde hair that touched her shoulders, and she was wearing a thick silver watch. She had long, curly eyelashes. I figured I'd better say something.

"I'm Foster McFee," I said. "I've never heard of you before, but my mama *loves* your movies." Macon made a noise, but I kept on going. "If you don't mind me saying, you look exactly like I thought an older actress would look. I've never once been close to anyone famous." Miss Charleena studied my socks. Both my big toes were sticking out. "I'm kind of new to town, and I appreciate being able to meet you. It's an honor."

Macon scurried like a squirrel. "Miss Charleena,

can I get you some tea and toast or some—"

She said, "Where are you from, Miss Foster McFee?"

"Memphis."

"Elvis still alive and well?"

"Well, he's dead, Miss Charleena, but his career keeps right on going."

"We can only pray for that longevity."

"Yes, ma'am. I do."

The little white dogs ran through the doggy door and wagged their tails.

"Hi there, sweet things." Miss Charleena patted them. She turned to Macon. "You go about your duties now."

Macon looked like he was going to bust open. "I . . . I . . . I will."

She walked slowly out of the room with the dogs following her. Her high heels made a *click click* sound.

"She doesn't look like she's dying to me," I whispered to Macon.

From the other room I heard, "Don't be so sure, darlin'."

★ ★ ★

"Okay, Foster, *first* you have to be totally careful about what you say in this house because Miss Charleena is *always* listening."

"I wish you'd told me that."

"I'm telling you now."

We were standing in what Macon called "The Great Hall" that had pictures and movie posters of Miss Charleena's career. He pointed to a picture of Miss Charleena hanging off the side of a ship in a long dress.

"This was her breakout role. She played a doctor's wife who got sick on a ship and died. She studied the frustration of being the wife of a doctor, with all the calls in the middle of the night and everything. She got letters from doctor's wives who said she got it just right."

"You mean dying?"

"I *mean* the whole thing—all the little movements and looks that an actor uses to create a character. She knows a lot about the world, Foster."

I stopped at a picture of Miss Charleena in a white coat examining a little boy. "She won an Emmy and a Golden Globe for playing Dr. Melinda Hutter on *Last Hope*. She was much beloved." He put his hand over his heart.

I smiled. "Do you have a crush on her?"

Macon's face went raspberry. *"No,"* he sputtered, *"of course not.* I can't believe you would say something like that!" He looked away. "I work for her and she's a great actress and it's nothing more than that, absolutely nothing. I can't believe you would think that!"

That means yes.

Macon pointed stiffly to another picture. "And here's one of her first roles. She was being chased by international criminals through the streets of Paris." He stopped at a movie poster of Miss Charleena standing by an elephant, surrounded by kids. "This is when she played a teacher in India. It's my favorite." Macon studied the picture. "Not everyone understands her, but I do."

I didn't see Miss Charleena again that day.

I straightened things in her kitchen as Macon watered her garden. My brain was making lists of everything to tell Mama. I looked inside her cookie jar, even though I wasn't supposed to touch anything. All she had were Ho Hos and Ding Dongs. I was not impressed. I had Foster's Best Brownie Cookies with Toasted Walnuts back in the Bullet, but no one was dying for any details about my life.

Not yet, at least.

This kitchen was huge—she had a silver stove, a double refrigerator, a wide-mouth toaster, and a blue food processor. In a glass case were blue-and-white dishes. All the wood was white. Shiny pots hung by the oven—they looked like they'd never been used. She had a work island just like Sonny Kroll has in his kitchen. The windows were big, too, but all the curtains were closed.

Someday I'm going to have a kitchen like this where I'll film my TV show. I'll roll out of bed, have my hair and makeup done, and get down to making food that will touch hearts.

I looked around and giggled. "Today on *Cooking with Foster*," I said quietly, "we're going to be visiting kitchens of the stars. But you want to remember that these people put their pants on one leg at a time, just like you do. Of course, their pants cost a lot more than yours, so remember that, too." I walked to the stove smiling just as Macon came in.

"I've got to feed the dogs, Foster, and then I'm done."

"Take your time," I told him. I could stay here forever. Macon chopped up chicken breast and bacon, which didn't look half bad, and filled their little gold bowls. He motioned me out the door. I waved good-bye to the kitchen.

That's it until next time on *Cooking with Foster*.

★ ★ ★

Macon and I walked down the hill, past a little stream, past a sign that I couldn't read. When I'm famous, I'm going to have people around me who do the reading.

"It meant a lot to Miss Charleena that I brought you," he said.

You could have fooled me. "Do famous people come to see her?"

"No one comes." Macon kicked a stone out of the way. "She came here to get away from people."

She did that, all right.

Macon stared through the trees to the prison below. The long, gray buildings looked creepy from above. "It opened two Christmases ago."

"That's a weird time to open a prison."

"Some of the town ladies decorated a tree and put it at the front gate. They were celebrating how the prison promised to bring all these new jobs to town. That's how I'm going to begin my movie—with a picture of the Christmas tree." Macon threw a stone and scared a squirrel. "People shouldn't make promises they can't keep."

I nodded.

"There's one thousand four hundred and eleven inmates in that place, Foster."

I thought about what it might be like with all those bad guys in one place. At my old school in Memphis, all the mean kids sat together in the lunchroom. Believe me, you didn't go near that table.

We headed down the hill.

"I put up signs around town saying I needed to talk to people about my movie, and not one person called," Macon said quietly.

We passed another sign I couldn't read. "Was that one of your signs?"

He looked at me strangely. "That says, 'Keep out— private property.'"

I walked faster. "I couldn't see it."

He caught up. "I just want people to take me seriously."

"Macon, you're the most serious boy on earth."

His eyes lit up. "I was even a serious baby. I had serious pets like snails and lizards. Look, you can help me make my movie."

"I don't know anything about making movies."

"You can be my assistant."

"I don't know how to—"

"Assistants go for coffee, but since I'm not drinking that yet, you can nod and take notes."

I'm not good at taking notes. "That's okay, Macon, I—"

"No, it's perfect." He grabbed my arm.

I tried to shake it free.

"It's only for a little while until my financing comes in, Foster. Then you can be the associate producer."

Twelve

PERSEVERANCE WILSON WAS sitting on the steps of the Church of God FOR SALE with her head bowed like she was praying.

"I don't think we should interrupt," I whispered, but Macon walked up to her anyway.

"Mrs. Wilson," he began, "could I ask you a few questions about the prison?"

She looked up. "I have a complicated relationship with that place."

"Take that down," Macon told me. I didn't write anything, but I did nod.

"I remember the dark day when the penitentiary opened," she said. "We had all those buses of prisoners coming through. It was an eerie feeling, like our town was never going to be the same."

I was doodling on the notepad to look busy, trying

to remember everything she said. "People were stressed, alarms were going off, guards were driving around town wearing mirrored sunglasses so you couldn't see their eyes." She shook her head. "But I got to thinking—what do you do when something you don't want and can't push away comes into your life?

"My husband used to say, sometimes the best thing you can do is the last thing you want to do." She laughed. "So we started the Helping Hands House."

"What's that?" I asked.

Macon glared at me. I guess assistants aren't supposed to ask questions.

She smoothed out her flowered skirt. "It's just a run-down building, child, but we give families a place to stay for a few days when they come to visit their loved ones in prison. Some of them have to travel a long way, and it's an expensive journey, so we do what we can."

"That's nice," I said, and doodled some more as Garland ran up, sweaty and breathing hard, and looking really good for a sweaty, breathless person.

"Hey," he said smiling.

"Hey." I grinned back.

Macon moved between us. "We're working here."

Garland looked around. "What are you doing?"

Macon rose up on his toes. "Exploring injustice. It's a major theme in documentary films."

Garland bent over, panting. "Sounds good."

"How'd the run feel today?" Percy asked him.

"Better. Except for the hill. I hate that hill."

"See how far you can go with it," she told him.

Garland smiled bright and drank some water. "You guys need help exploring injustice?"

Macon looked at my notepad and saw the doodle.

It was a good doodle, but . . .

"*What is this?*" he hollered.

My face got hot.

"I remember everything she said, Macon, it's how I—"

"I didn't ask you to remember! I asked you to write!"

Everyone was looking at me.

"You didn't write down one word of that interview!"

"Kids, put a lid on this," Perseverance Wilson warned.

"You're fired," Macon said to me.

"*You can't fire me. I quit!*"

And I was out of there. I tore off down the road.

Maybe the shame couldn't catch me.

Maybe if I ran fast enough, I wouldn't cry.

But I couldn't run faster than Garland. He caught

up with me. "Hey, Foster. What just happened?"

I couldn't look at him. "I can't talk about it!"

"That's okay, I just—"

It's not okay! I ran down the road toward Fish Hardware and Mama.

I'm not stupid, I told myself. *There's all kinds of things I can do.*

But enough of me must be stupid if I'm twelve years old and I can't take notes.

My stomach muscles were cramping. I could see the hardware store ahead. I stopped running and walked toward it. The front window had paint cans, fishing poles, and an ugly hose.

A woman's hand reached into the window. I recognized that hand. Now more of her was in the window; she was taking out the paint cans.

"Mama!" I shouted, but she couldn't hear me. I knocked on the glass, and you should have seen her grin. Mama was always glad to see me.

She posed like she was a mannequin; then she picked up a paintbrush and held it up like she was the Statue of Liberty. I started laughing. Her eyes followed something coming up next to me.

"I'm sorry I fired you." It was Macon.

I turned away. "You didn't fire me. I quit."

"I'm sorry I fired you so you had to quit."

He looked at Mama posed in the window. "What's your mother doing?"

"Working."

Two men in gray uniforms were cleaning up the empty lot next door, picking up trash and putting it in bags. A man wearing mirrored sunglasses watched them.

"Those men are from the prison work release program," Macon said.

The man in mirrored sunglasses shouted, "Duke, get those bags and we'll be done."

Duke got the bags and threw them in a Dumpster near where we were standing. A bird was singing in a tree. "Sing it sweet, bird," Duke told it. "You're free."

A noise sounded like a distant siren. A large woman headed toward us.

"Oh, boy." Macon cleared his throat. "Mrs. Dupree, how are you?"

"If the sound of that prison alarm isn't a call to right living, then I don't know what is. Just think what a life of crime can cost you. Locked up. No place to go. All your freedoms taken away."

"I was thinking about that earlier, Mrs. Dupree." Macon pushed me forward. "This is my friend Foster."

"How do you do, dear?"

I've been better. "Fine, thank you, ma'am."

Mama winked at me from the window. Mrs. Dupree stared at her. I winked back. "That's my mama."

"Really . . ."

"We're new in town."

Macon had a strange expression on his face. "Foster, Mrs. Dupree is the—"

"You must be looking forward to starting school, dear."

"Oh, no ma'am. Not one bit."

Macon made a noise deep in his throat.

Mrs. Dupree stopped short. All of her seemed gray— gray hair, gray face, gray eyes. She took another glance at Mama and hurried off.

Macon threw his arms in the air. *"She's the middle school principal, Foster!"*

I closed my eyes. Principals should have to wear a bell around their necks to warn kids they're coming!

We *so* cannot stay here.

★ ★ ★

I told Mama what happened and she *laughed*.

"We have to move," I shouted.

She smiled. "There might be another solution."

"I'm not going to that woman's school!"

"Maybe it's a good school."

A voice from the back of Fish Hardware said, "It's a pretty good school."

I moved closer to Mama and whispered, "I'd have to dye my hair and wear a mask so she wouldn't recognize me!"

"She'd recognize you." Amy walked from the back carrying a screwdriver. "Look at this. It's electric." The screwdriver whirred. "No more wrist strain. It's a must-have cool tool, don't you think?" Another whirr. "I want to put it on sale this Saturday and have free coffee and cookies to bring people in."

Mr. Fish popped his head up from an aisle. "In this economy no one is giving anything away free."

"Daddy, we have to listen to our customers. They want more."

"We sell hardware. Let them get their own coffee." His head went back down.

Amy sighed and looked at me. "Sorry. You were

saying you'd have to dye your hair and wear a mask so Mrs. Dupree wouldn't recognize you."

It sounded stupid when she said it.

Mama put her hand on my shoulder. "And I was about to say, I have every confidence Foster can handle whatever comes."

Amy nodded.

Then Mama said we were staying here for the time being and I should feel free to make the best of it.

Amy nodded again.

Making the best of it was something Mama had been shoving down my throat since I could talk. She went back to clearing out the front window. Amy walked toward the back.

I had to do what I'd done in Memphis. There was no other way.

Thirteen

I'M HERE, WORLD, and I've got baked goods!

I stood outside Angry Wayne's Bar and Grill holding tight to my Bake and Take. Inside this carrier were six chocolate chip muffins and six vanilla cupcakes.

A sleepy dog lay by the screen door. Two red-headed boys were chasing something in the parking lot, laughing. I was about to go in when I heard a man shout, "You want to get me good and riled?" Then something hit the wall and a buzzer went off.

I jumped back. *"What was that?"*

"Our poppa," the taller red-headed boy said.

A man in a uniform, wearing mirrored sunglasses, walked out. He held the door open. "Going in?" he asked me.

I nodded and walked inside.

Three men and a lady sat at the counter; not one

of them looked happy. Stuffed fish hung on the wall. They didn't look happy either. There wasn't much to this long, thin place. The sausages on the grill looked good, though.

"You know what they did now, Wayne?" one of the men asked.

A man with red hair was standing at the grill. "Can my heart take it, Clay?"

"The prison's putting Tommy out of business. All those promises they were going to buy from him—just a pack of lies."

Wayne's face got pink and splotchy. He reached down, got a rubber ball, and threw it at a buzzer on the wall that buzzed loud. The ball dropped into a net below. "They can't do that!"

"They're doing it, boy."

"They're doing it," the men and lady said.

I stepped forward, tried to have stage presence like Mama taught me. "Excuse me."

They all turned to look. Angry Wayne flipped the sausages. "You lost?"

Sure feels that way, mister. I missed Marietta Morningstar and her little pink bake shop.

"I'm new in town and I'm a baker and I was

wondering, sir, if I could help you in the kitchen. You wouldn't have to pay me or anything. I'd just like to learn. I did this in Memphis."

"Don't hire children," he said.

"I understand. I just want to help."

"Don't need no help."

I looked around at the dead fish hanging on the wall. This seemed to be a popular decorating choice in Culpepper. My eyes stopped on a scratched, plastic box with boring sweet rolls inside. *I'd say you need help, sir.*

"I brought some samples. I've got chocolate chip muffins and vanilla cupcakes." I opened the Bake and Take. "Would you like to try one, Mr. Wayne?"

He sniffed, which might mean yes. The lady's eyes popped. "I haven't had a cupcake in I don't know when," she said. "Are these free?"

"They're free today, but Mr. Wayne, I don't want to be a bother." I figured he wasn't a cupcake man, so I handed him a muffin.

He held it up and studied it. This is what food people do.

"I use a touch of corn flour," I told him. "Makes it chewy."

He took a bite, and I saw a little sparkle in his eyes.

He took his time chewing it—it was like he was moving it from side to side in his mouth. I've seen people tasting wine like that on the Food Network. He took a gulp of coffee, took another bite.

"You made this?"

I nodded. "It's got butter and—"

"I know what it's got. What else you make?"

"I make pumpkin muffins, apple cinnamon ones, banana bread, pineapple upside-down cake, cupcakes—"

"Vanilla cupcakes," the woman whispered.

"I ain't deaf, Betty."

"I need a cupcake." Betty grabbed one and took a bite. "Oh, now I'm in heaven!"

The two men at the counter each took a muffin and gobbled it down. Betty licked every last bit of frosting off the paper liner like a little kid and put her hand over her heart. Wayne turned back to the grill and fried up some onions.

A man who looked like a policeman came in and sat at the counter. "What's good today?"

"Cupcakes," Betty told him.

"Really?" He looked at what I'd brought. "How much?"

"Dollar," Wayne said.

I coughed and motioned Wayne over. "You should charge more, sir."

"Dollar fifty, Sheriff. Not a penny less for fresh baked."

"Gimme two."

I handed him two. They were gone fast. "This is a fine cupcake." He brushed crumbs off his pants. "Heard Zeke got jumped at the prison. Wasn't paying attention."

"Gotta pay attention," the others said.

I looked down and couldn't believe what I saw. A huge spider with a black hairy body was crawling across the floor toward me!

I jumped back. *"Get it away from me! Get it away!"*

"Oh, Lord," Wayne said.

The people at the counter shook their heads. The red-headed boys opened the screen door, laughing.

"Gotcha good!" the taller one said.

What?

"Barry and Larry, take that tarantula outside pronto!" Wayne shouted.

Tarantula? I'd seen the Nature Network enough to know what that meant.

The other boy picked up the tarantula. "Come on, Jim Bob, off you go."

"Works from twenty-five feet," the other said happily, and showed me the remote control.

A remote-controlled tarantula? I tried to catch a normal breath.

"*Outside!*" Wayne yelled.

The boys ran off. I closed my Bake and Take.

"Don't get your britches in a bunch," Wayne said to me.

I gulped and nodded. He went back to grilling. Betty reached for a cupcake.

"That'll be a dollar fifty," Wayne told her.

"It was free a minute ago."

"These were free?" the sheriff asked.

Wayne held out his hand for the money. "I'm a businessman, Betty."

She put seventy-five cents in his hand and gave seventy-five cents to me.

"What's this?" Wayne demanded.

"Good business." Betty ate that cupcake like it was the last one on earth.

"You want me to bring more tomorrow, Mr. Wayne?"

Everyone at the counter nodded.

Betty raised her eyebrows. "How much will you be paying this girl, Wayne?"

He thought about that. "Twenty-five percent of the take."

Betty shook her head. "Not less than fifty."

"I got overhead, woman!"

Betty glared at him until he muttered, "All right. Fifty percent. We'll try it for one day."

Whoo hoo!

I'm a professional baker! At least till tomorrow. Longer, maybe, if I don't mess up. I ran out the door, hugging my Bake and Take.

"Can I have a muffin for my tarantula?" the taller red-headed boy asked.

"No!"

He pressed the remote and the tarantula's eyes lit up. "You want to pet him?"

I jumped over that thing and headed down the road. I had big-time baking to do.

Fourteen

WHAT I CAN absolutely tell you about these chocolate chip muffins that I just baked for Angry Wayne is that they are the best ones of my career—fat, buttery, golden brown, and a little crusty on top. I tried to imagine them going into the deepest recesses of Angry Wayne's heart, but that was hard to picture. I put them on a rack to cool and thought about Eddington Carver.

He and I were the king and queen of school bake sales. Eddington sold his enormous raspberry rolls that were so light and sweet you'd eat them until you got sick. I brought my triple chocolate blowout cupcakes that had cocoa, chocolate chips, and chocolate sprinkles on top. The smartest thing I ever did in sixth grade was give Mrs. Ritter a free cupcake. It was the only time she smiled at me. I think it might be why I passed sixth grade.

I looked at the book on the table tucked under the Bullet's round window. It was Mama's favorite book of all time, *To Kill a Mockingbird.* Don't go thinking I could read the title. I couldn't. It had one of those trick titles, because it didn't have a bird anywhere in the story. Last year Mama read the book to me. It was about life in the South and how unfair some white people were to a black man, so unfair that they accused him of doing something he didn't do. Mama said the story is about courage and fighting for justice, but I think it's about what hate can do.

I held the book; 281 pages, all small print, no pictures. It was almost falling apart, too, because Mama had read it so much. Books were Mama's friends.

I needed a best friend in this town.

Eddington moved to Texas the day after school was out. I baked him butterscotch muffins to eat in the car. "Someday," he told me, "crowds of people are going to line up to buy this muffin."

He gave me his number, but I lost it. I wished I could call him and tell him that I got a job as a baker for a day.

There was a knock at the door. It was Kitty. She held out her phone. "It's that boy, Macon. He says it's an emergency."

I took the phone. "Hi . . ." was as far as I got.

"I'm desperate, Foster! I've got a fever and I'm coughing and I can't go to Miss Charleena's for a few days. I need you to go there and do my chores. I called Amy first, but she said she couldn't handle the stress."

This sounded like a *bad* idea. "I have to ask my mom."

"You have to do this, Foster, or Miss Charleena will hire another kid and I'll never be able to buy a movie camera! My entire life will be ruined! You're my only hope!"

* * *

Mama said, "Of course, what an opportunity," and that's why I am standing in front of Macon's house. It was set in the back of the woods hidden from the road. There were lots of houses here, but Macon's house looked like people had been adding onto it without thinking. There was a section painted yellow and another painted blue, the roof had three different colors, a door leaned against a tree, a curling stairway went up to the roof.

Macon opened a window. "I called Miss Charleena and told her you were coming."

"What did she say?"

"She made a sound."

"What kind of a sound?"

"Like a grunt. Knock at the back door and she'll let you in. She's really very nice when you get to know her, although that can take a long time. I'm sorry I can't come out; I've got hives."

"That's okay."

"There's nothing about hives that's okay, Foster!" He started coughing like he was going to die.

"Feel better!"

I walked past flat-roof houses and trailers with broken-down cars in front of them. Clothes flapped on lines. I walked past FOOD and the Church of God FOR SALE and saw a woman and a man get out of a car. They walked toward the church.

"It won't take much to knock this place down," the woman said.

The man looked at the church and nodded. They headed up the stairs.

"Lots of parking, too," she mentioned, and unlocked the big lock on the front door.

They went inside.

"Lord, give me strength." Perseverance Wilson marched up like she had to defend all that was right and true. Garland was behind her.

"Who's that lady?" I asked.

"The *Realtor*," Garland explained as his mother headed up the steps. "The guy is from the Taco Terrific restaurant chain."

"They're terrible."

Percy shouted, "They want to put one here on sacred ground." She opened the church door and yelled. "Did you folks know about the rodent problem?"

Garland looked like he wanted to punch something. I said, "This must be hard for you."

"My dad built this church."

I could hear Percy's voice: "And when you folks get to the basement, be sure to get a good look at the photos of my late, great husband, our founding pastor. His heart is in these walls!"

★ ★ ★

Angry Wayne had Barry and Larry out back by their earlobes. "You scared that lady so bad with that blasted tarantula, she started choking!"

I left the muffins and cupcakes at the counter with Betty. "It's a good batch," I told her.

A man wearing mirrored sunglasses came over. "Those the ones you were talking about?"

Betty put them in a container. "They are."

"I'll take two."

That's a good start. I headed out the door to Miss Charleena's and almost got knocked over by Angry Wayne storming in.

"Hello, sir."

He didn't say anything.

"I brought the muffins and the—"

He hit the buzzer on the wall and stood behind the grill.

"It's my best batch ever," I whispered, and went outside where Barry and Larry were trying to get their tarantula to climb a rock.

"We're saving up for a black widow spider," the short boy said. "Then we'll rule."

"Are you Barry or Larry?"

"Larry."

The taller one stepped forward. "And that would make me . . . ?"

"Difficult," I said.

Larry broke up at that.

I headed to Marigold Hill, Miss Charleena, and who knew what else.

Fifteen

I PUT ON my TV smile and knocked at the back door.

Miss Charleena opened it, not smiling. She was wearing a bright red shirt, white jeans, and a necklace with a silver circle.

I gulped. "Hi, Miss Charleena."

She didn't say hello. She gave me a long list—two pages stapled together on pretty blue paper.

Not a list! Just tell me!

"I'm feeling weak," she said. "I'm going to lie down. I *do not* like being disturbed." She walked away, her heels click clicking.

I looked at the list and my mind closed up. I could make out a few of the words like *dogs, food,* and *don't.*

Don't what?

Feed the dogs?

Feed the dogs food?

I pictured Macon getting fired and never getting his movie camera, all because I couldn't read.

I'm so dead.

The phone rang and rang. Am I supposed to answer it? It stopped ringing, then it started again. Maybe Miss Charleena was too sick to answer it. I reached for the phone. "Miss Charleena's house. This is Foster speaking."

"*This* is Charleena Hendley. Why do I not hear the sounds of you getting down to work?"

I gulped.

"Surely, I've given you enough to do."

"Yes ma'am, the thing is . . ."

"*What* is the thing?"

How do I tell her? "I'm having a little trouble reading your handwriting. It's real pretty and all."

"Oh, for heaven's sake!" She slammed the phone down.

Now what do I do? I didn't hear anything for the longest time, then Miss Charleena's click clicking sounds were coming toward the kitchen. I stood at attention as she entered. She looked at me, not impressed. "*Here* is a computer printout of your tasks." She handed me a sheet of paper that was plain as anything, if you're a reader.

I took a big breath. "I want to do everything like you

want it, Miss Charleena, and I appreciate you trusting me in your house. Could we just go over this list and then you can get back to resting?"

She looked at me for a minute. I didn't dare breathe. Then she sat at the table and began to read from the list, but not in a normal person's voice, like the great actress she was.

"Feed the dogs, Foster. The food is in the cabinet above the refrigerator. They like some chicken breast chopped fine mixed in with their food and a little bacon or shaved parmesan on top. That's in the refrigerator."

My amazing memory clicked this into place.

"Are we clear so far?"

I nodded. She looked at me like she was trying to figure something out. "Why don't you read the second item?" She pushed the list toward me.

I pushed it back. "I'd like you to do it."

She held it out to me. "Go ahead."

I looked at the mess of words and shook my head. "I wish you'd read it, Miss Charleena. I didn't bring my glasses."

She looked at me again. Then she read, "Water the plants outside, but only at the roots. If you water the petals they will get brown and I will not be happy."

"I want you to be happy."

"Good." She handed me the list.

"Is that it?" I asked.

She put her fingernail on some words. "What does that say?"

I sucked in air. "Boy, I wish I'd brought my glasses."

She studied me. "Feed the parakeet from the box of birdseed in the closet near the refrigerator. Do you see that?"

I nodded.

"You're sure you see that?"

"Yes, ma'am. As plain as anything."

"Why don't you do those three things and then we'll go over the rest of the list." She sounded almost nice when she said it. I breathed easier. She grabbed a Ho Ho from the counter and left the room.

I went to get the dog food and found a can opener after opening close to every drawer in the kitchen. I couldn't find the chicken at first and was thinking spiteful thoughts about spoiled dogs who only eat fancy food. I finally found the chicken and parmesan cheese. By mistake I dropped the chicken on the floor and the two dogs ran in and tore it to shreds. They didn't need it chopped at all.

"That's enough, you guys." I tried to clean up the chicken and got growled at. I sliced off a hunk of parmesan, threw it in the corner, and the dogs ran after it. I picked up what was left of the chicken. "Okay. You've had your lunch."

I wish I could just bake for Miss Charleena, since I was not very good at this job.

I cleaned up the floor, went to the closet, and looked everywhere for the birdseed, but I couldn't find it. I went back to check the list; the words blurred together. I looked for the bird I was supposed to feed and I couldn't find that either!

I heard the click clicking coming closer.

Miss Charleena came in, leaned against the wall, and crossed her arms. "Well?" she asked.

I smiled with everything I had. "I fed the dogs and they really loved how I did it. But I can't find the birdseed." This next part was harder to admit. "Or the bird."

She stood there.

"There is no bird," she said quietly.

"What?"

"There is no bird." She studied my face. "You can't read. Can you?"

Sixteen

I STOOD THERE, hot with shame. I wanted to run, but my feet felt nailed to the floor.

I wanted to scream, *Hey, good trick, Miss Charleena. You really fooled me.*

"I asked you a question," she said softly.

She could play all her tricks and games on me, she could stand there like she'd won, but I didn't have to answer her.

"There's lots of people who have trouble reading," she said, like I'd been living in a cave and didn't know that.

I looked down at the dogs' golden dishes. I felt my face get tight and my jaw get hard.

Miss Charleena walked over to the refrigerator, poured herself a glass of milk, and stirred chocolate syrup into it for the longest time. It seemed like the sound of that stirring spoon was in front of a microphone.

I think the chocolate is mixed in now. Just drink it!

"I've gotta go, Miss Charleena."

"Not before I tell you something."

But I headed out the door, down the path, tears shooting from my eyes.

"Foster! Wait!"

I ran as fast as my skinny legs could go, tripped over a rock in the road, and fell flat on my face, scraping my knees bloody, spitting mud from my mouth.

I hated Miss Charleena for tricking me. I hated Macon for getting sick. I hated Mama for bringing us here.

I got up and ran some more.

"Foster," Mrs. Ritter, my main sixth-grade teacher, had said to me, "do you understand that you are graduating by the skin of your teeth?"

I didn't know teeth had skin, but I didn't want to get anything more wrong at this school, so I said, "Yes, ma'am."

"I don't see the value of having you repeat sixth grade again."

I was with her on that.

"But I cannot stress the need for you to develop better work habits, because if you do not, young lady, your life will be limited beyond what you can even imagine."

I saw a sign up ahead, but I couldn't read it. I felt like there was a sign hanging on me.

Limited.

Challenged.

Stupid.

Lazy.

I sat down in the dirt and cried, as lost as any girl ever was in this world.

★ ★ ★

I don't know how long I sat there. I wasn't sure which way was home.

Did I head up or down? Miss Charleena lived on top of the hill. I didn't want to see her ever again, but I didn't have much choice. I headed up until I saw her big gray house.

I knocked at the back door. I rang the doorbell. I shouted, "It's me, Foster!"

Finally, Miss Charleena opened the door. "What happened to you?"

I smoothed back my hair. "I fell."

She looked at me like she had X-ray vision.

"I got lost," I added. "And I spent some time being upset."

"Let's get some bandages on those knees."

"I don't mean to be any trouble."

She made a noise and pointed to the bathroom.

I went inside. It was beautiful blue with white trim and a silver mirror on the wall. First thing I did was get blood on the white rug. I ran the water and soaped up my knees. I patted them dry and got blood on the towel. My hands had cuts, too. I washed my face.

"You all right in there?"

"Yes."

I put ointment on my knees and hands and put bandages over them. I found a comb and tried to fix my hair. The comb broke—my hair can do that. I walked out holding the rug and the towel.

"How much do you like these, Miss Charleena?"

"Why?"

I showed her the blood.

She sighed and looked at my shoes. I'd forgotten to take them off, but she didn't mention it. "I'm not much of a cook, Foster, but I could make you a hamburger."

I was hungry. "That'd be good."

I sat on a stool in the kitchen as she took out hamburger meat and pressed it hard into a patty. I cleared my throat. "If you don't mind me saying, if you pat the meat gently it'll stay juicier."

"I didn't know that." She looked at the patty. "How do I undo it?"

"Well." I went over and tore the meat into little sections and patted them together lightly.

She got out a frying pan and turned it to high.

"Uh, Miss Charleena. It's better to cook a burger not quite so hot."

"You've got a lot of opinions on hamburgers, Foster McFee."

"I watch the Food Network a lot."

"I never watch it."

I could tell. "Sonny Kroll is my favorite chef. I've been watching him for years. My specialty is baking—cupcakes, butterscotch muffins."

"Butterscotch muffins!"

"These muffins open hearts," I told her.

"What do you need to make butterscotch muffins?"

"Butter, brown sugar, vanilla, flour, salt, eggs, pecans, and butterscotch pudding mix."

She wrote that down. "I'll make sure I have that

when you come tomorrow. I'm guessing you'd like to make your own burger."

I really would. I went over to the stove and turned down the heat a little. "Do you have some oil?"

She handed it to me. I spread a little in the pan. "That gets it nice and crunchy on the outside." Miss Charleena was sitting on the stool watching. "And you've got to wait till you see the burger getting cooked through just like this. That's when you flip it, not before. You've got to be patient." She made a noise again. I put salt and pepper on the top.

Miss Charleena got me a hamburger bun; I split it and put it in the pan with the burger to get it toasty. She put barbecue sauce on the counter. I layered my burger on the toasted bun, put the sauce on.

"That looks good," she said.

I handed it to her. "Here, you eat this one. I'll make another."

She took a bite. "This is a fine burger. Mine always tastes dry."

I made another patty and put it in the pan.

She smiled. "Where do you keep your recipes, Foster?"

I knew where she was going with that question. "In my head."

She nodded and ate the burger. "I used to have a terrible time with reading. If I hadn't gotten help, I wouldn't have been able to be an actor. It was the hardest thing I ever did."

What did she just say?

She finished her burger. "Learning how to read just about split my brain open, but it was worth it."

My brain had enough splits in it already. I flipped my burger.

"I used to do what you did, Foster—say I'd lost my reading glasses, ask people to read to me. I kept the secret for a long time, but it's hard to live like that."

If she knew how hard it was, then why did she trick me?

"I could try to help you."

Was she kidding?

I've tried to read, and the words turn to smudges on a page. I've tried sounding them out. I've tried memorizing them.

My burger was done.

I put the burger in a bun, heaped on barbecue sauce, and wasn't sure what was happening in my heart.

"I could maybe teach you to cook better, Miss Charleena."

She looked at me. She had the longest eyelashes. "Many have tried to teach me to cook, Foster, and they have failed. What makes you think you can do it?"

"I don't know. I just love it, I guess, and I want other people to love it, too."

"Why do you love it?"

I didn't know how to tell her that cooking saved me.

"I'd really like to know, Foster."

"Miss Charleena, in school I feel like an all-out loser, but when I cook, I feel like I can beat the world."

She smiled. "Maybe we could work out a deal. You give me some cooking lessons and I'll help you with your reading."

I wasn't sure I wanted to combine something I loved so much with something I hated.

My mind raced back to sixth grade and Mrs. Ritter making me read out loud in front of the entire class. I'd be tripping over words as the other kids smirked.

Concentrate, she'd say.

I was doing that!

Look at it harder!

You're taking up everyone's time, young lady!

Then don't call on me, okay? Just leave me alone!

I'm not going through that again. No way.

"I'll give you cooking lessons, Miss Charleena, but I'm not up to reading right now. School's hard enough without having it spill into summer."

"I understand."

I ate my burger, then she handed me the phone. "Call your mother. I'll drive you home."

I punched in Mama's number and got her voice mail. "Hi, Mama, it's me. Miss Charleena is driving me home. Oh . . . and the bleeding's stopped. You don't have to worry."

Miss Charleena reached for her keys and headed for the door. "One more thought on reading. What if it turns out you can do it?"

I looked away. It would mean a lot. More than I know how to say.

Seventeen

SOMEDAY I'M GOING to have a car like this.

The wind whooshed through my hair as Miss Charleena zoomed down the road in her baby blue convertible. We passed the prison. Tall towers stood behind the razor wire fence.

"I was in a prison movie once," Miss Charleena told me. "I played the wife of a murderer. I talked to women whose husbands were in jail, I visited prisons so I could get into my role. And you know the number one thing that helped me find my character?"

"What?" I wasn't sure what she meant about finding her character.

"I went back to a time in my life when I felt scared, lonely, forgotten, and misunderstood, and I used those memories to create my character." She turned down the road to Kitty and Lester's house. "I was up for an Oscar for that role."

"Wow, Miss Charleena."

"I've been nominated twice, actually; never won."

"So you had to sit there smiling when someone else won?" Mama let me stay up to see the Oscar show a few times.

"My face was hurting from the fake smile, and both times my dress was too tight. But I went home and hugged my Emmy and my Golden Globe and felt better."

I used to hug Daddy's pillowcase when things hurt.

She drove past the broken fence, pulled into the driveway, and stopped her little car next to the big tow truck. "Kitty and Lester pulled my car out of a ditch once."

"How did it get in a ditch?"

She sighed. "Let's just say I wasn't doing too well when I first moved back home."

"It must have been hard to come here after being in Hollywood."

"Foster, at that time in my life, any place I lived was guaranteed to be hard."

Just then Mama ran out of the Bullet dressed like she was going to meet a queen. She had all her makeup on, her hair was wound up on her head, and she was wearing a fancy top, her best pants, and high heels.

"*Ms. Hendley*, I can't tell you what an honor it is to meet you. I've seen all your movies. You've made me laugh and cry." She shook Miss Charleena's hand and said to me, "What's this about the bleeding?"

"I fell on my face. That's all."

Mama looked at my bandaged knees.

"You've got a fine girl here," Miss Charleena said.

"Thank you kindly. Every movie you've made I've seen at least three times." Mama was talking a little too loud.

"I appreciate it."

"And here you are your very self!"

"Here I am, but I must be going."

"Of course you must. Be going, that is." I'd never seen Mama like this.

"It's a pleasure. Is it all right for her to come by tomorrow?"

"Absolutely. Of course. No problem. Thank you for driving her home."

I got out of the car. "Miss Charleena, that thing you said about finding your character—what did you mean?"

"An actor can't play a part well unless you understand

who your character is—how they feel, where they're scared, what makes them tick, what makes them strong or weak. I'd find those places in my life where I felt like that and I'd let them come out in the acting."

"I can see why you almost got an Oscar."

"Almost. Not quite."

"But you might still get one. I mean, you're old, but not ancient."

"Foster!" Mama shouted.

"Careful, darlin'. Aging is a serious matter in Hollywood."

"I can't wait to get older!"

She revved the motor. "There will be a point, I assure you, when that will change." She tooted her horn and drove off.

We waved good-bye. Mama put her hand over her heart. "I can't believe I just met Charleena Hendley."

I looked at Mama's fancy outfit. "Did you wear that to work?"

"Don't be fresh!" Then she grabbed my arm. "Tell me *everything*."

★ ★ ★

"We're having fun, right?"

Sonny Kroll shouted it in his TV kitchen.

"Right!" I shouted back.

"Today we're making . . . oh, I don't know if you can handle it."

I laughed. "I can. . . ."

His face got close to the screen, so close I wanted to touch his forehead.

"We're making the moistest, proudest cupcakes you've ever tasted!"

I'm ready.

"Now I want you to commit this to memory, because there's some people out there that think a cupcake is some little, dinky thing."

Lester walked by. I was sitting on his couch watching the show. "Who's that?"

"Sonny Kroll," I told him.

Lester sat down to watch as Sonny put his hands on the counter and leaned forward. "There are three hard and fast rules for making a proper cupcake. Listen up for Kroll's Cupcake Commands. Number one—no cupcake shall be small. Number two—no cupcake shall have just a little frosting. And number three—no cupcake shall be eaten alone."

Lester chuckled.

"*Do you hear me?*" Sonny shouted. He'd been a

marine sergeant before he got his cooking show.

"We hear you!" Lester and I shouted back.

"We're going right to the powerhouse flavors here— chocolate and vanilla. And we'll be piling them higher and deeper. But first, you need to get your hands on the best cocoa you can find. . . ."

Sonny went through the ingredients, which I already had. He measured cake flour, cocoa, and one and a quarter teaspoons baking soda. "Make sure it's fresh."

He added one quarter teaspoon baking powder. "Mix all the dry ingredients in a bowl, and feel good about yourself because you're making something that's going to give a lot of people joy."

He got out another bowl and cracked three eggs into it. "Now add one and two thirds cups of sugar, a teaspoon of vanilla—real vanilla extract please. And beat that egg mixture for three minutes on high with your mixer, and as you do that it's going to get creamy and smooth. Now you reduce the speed to low, and hold on to your heart, folks, because here comes the secret ingredient. Mayonnaise. I can hear you groaning, but have I ever lied to you? The answer is *no, sir!* Don't go running off on me. Measure out one cup of mayo and add it to the batter and beat that stuff in until it's blended. Then you

get a cup and a third of water and add the flour mixture
to the egg mixture in batches—not all at once or it will
get lumpy. Put in about a fourth of the flour, then a
fourth of the water, and blend; do this four times and
you've got serious batter. Frosting alone does not make a
cupcake. We're building this baby from the ground up."

He put the batter in paper liners, filled it two thirds
full, and put it in the oven. "For twenty to twenty-five
minutes—don't overbake—that's an order."

"I'm so making these," I told Lester.

"Don't you need to write this down?"

I pointed to my head. "I remember everything."

"No kidding?"

Then Sonny showed the secret to his vanilla
cupcakes. "Sour cream," he whispered. "Only you and
me need to know this."

The cupcakes came out big, and he piled on the
frosting, put sprinkles on them. Then he put them in
a fancy carrier, much fancier than mine, got his helmet
from by the door, and headed outside. His motorcycle
was sitting there like always. He put the cupcakes in the
carrier behind the seat, climbed on the bike, and revved it.

"We're on this road together." And he zoomed off on
that thing.

"Marines always ate better than army," Lester mentioned. "That Sonny's a good man."

Someday, I hope, I'll be able to shake his hand and tell him all he's done for me.

"You ever write him a letter?" Lester asked.

"No."

"Maybe you should."

Believe me, Lester. If I could I would.

* * *

Mama let me stay up and make Sonny's mayonnaise cupcakes so I wouldn't forget the recipe. Once I get a recipe in my head and make it, I don't forget. Why this doesn't happen in school is one of life's big mysteries.

After one bite of this cupcake, I knew I'd never forget the recipe.

I was up early and rushed to get dressed so I could get to Miss Charleena's. I called Macon to see how he was feeling.

"Did you do everything at Miss Charleena's you needed to do yesterday?" he demanded.

"Everything."

"And was she happy? I mean, it's not always easy to tell."

"She was happy."

"How do you know?"

"She was nice, Macon. She was just nice."

"*Nice?*" He started coughing.

"I've got to go. Take care of yourself."

"Tell me more about the nice, Foster." Lots more coughing.

"We're learning to work together, you know?"

He didn't know, but I didn't have time to explain, and if I did have time, I'm not sure I could have done it.

It was a new day. I felt like I had cream filling inside me.

I packed up two chocolate mayonnaise cupcakes for Miss Charleena and headed for her house. When I turned up Marigold Hill, it seemed like all the birds were singing for me. I got to Miss Charleena's back door and knocked. I waited, knocked again. I rang the bell. Her car was in the driveway. Where was she?

Finally, Miss Charleena came to the door, but she looked different from how she did yesterday. Her hair was mussed, her face looked long and tired.

"Miss Charleena, are you okay?"

"The sickness has come back."

She walked out of the kitchen, down the hall, and left me standing there.

Eighteen

DR. WEBER WALKED down the long hall past all the pictures of Miss Charleena's most memorable movie moments. He knocked at her bedroom door. "What is it today, Charleena?"

"I'm dying," she said.

That sounded bad!

Dr. Weber went into her room and shut the door. I said a prayer to God that she'd be okay.

The door opened and Dr. Weber came out. He walked through the house, out to his car, and in a minute he came back lugging a machine "for oxygen." He wheeled it into her room.

I didn't know what to do, so I went back to the kitchen. The dogs, Tracy and Hepburn, walked in slowly. I knelt down and rubbed them.

"She'll be okay, you guys." They nuzzled my hand.

"She'll want to see you soon, I bet. I hope she'll want to see me."

Here we were in the beautiful kitchen and all the curtains were closed. On the counter were butter, brown sugar, vanilla, flour, and pecans. Not quite everything I needed to make butterscotch muffins.

"But, we're going to go with what we've got," I told the dogs. "I'm making brown sugar brownies." Sometimes the best thing a person can do in an emergency is bake.

I found a pan, turned the oven on to 350. The butter was soft; I creamed it with a wooden spoon, added brown sugar, and beat that together till it was fluffy. The fluffy part is important. I have very strong hands, which a good cook needs, because you're stirring and chopping all day. I added two eggs and vanilla and mixed that in. I put flour, salt, and baking powder in another bowl and stirred them together. I was careful to measure the baking powder, because if you put in too much, the brownies taste nasty and get holes inside them when they bake. I stirred in the flour combination and tried the batter. This recipe never fails.

I left a spoon with batter on a plate in case Miss Charleena got up from her sickness and needed a treat.

I put the batter in the pan, put the pan in the oven.

I told the dogs, "In fifteen minutes, this kitchen is going to smell like a celebration." One of the big things I've learned watching TV cooks is that they have confidence. If they said, "I don't know if this recipe's going to turn out," all over the world people would be clicking their TV remotes to off. If you want people to stay with you, act like you know what you're doing. There are lots of life lessons on the Food Network.

I fed Tracy and Hepburn, swept the back porch, and brought in the paper. I wasn't sure what the headline said, but I knew one word, WAR. My daddy told me once that he expected there would always be a war going on somewhere in the world. In fifth grade I did a shadow box on peace for Mr. Mackey's class. I made people out of popsicle sticks and colored their faces all the colors of people in the world. Everyone was wearing white, and they were standing together holding hands. My peace box was put on the front table in the school for everyone to see, until Ronny Mandolini smashed it with his fist.

I wiped the kitchen counters, cleaned the back door window, and took the brownies from the oven. Perfect. Miss Charleena needed to smell these.

I walked to her bedroom door and heard Dr. Weber say, "Charleena, in my professional opinion, you're breathing fine, as always."

"I can hardly get a breath," she insisted.

The phone rang and rang. Finally, I picked it up.

"Miss Charleena's residence. This is Foster speaking."

"Tell her Stan's on the line."

"She's with the doctor."

"Tell her," the man Stan insisted.

I walked back down the hall to the closed white door and knocked.

"Miss Charleena, Mr. Stan is on the line."

Her voice sounded small. "Tell him not now."

I put the phone to my ear and told him.

"Put her on, kid." He had a pushy voice.

"She can't talk right now. She's with the doctor."

"What did you say your name was?"

"Foster."

"Foster, let me tell you about life. There's life for regular people and there's life for Hollywood people. Are you following me?"

"Yessir."

"And the Hollywood life, Foster, goes like this.

Actors need agents to prevent them from driving their careers into a ditch."

Miss Charleena had mentioned being in a ditch, but I thought Kitty and Lester yanked her out.

"I'm Charleena's agent, Foster. I take calls for her, and sometimes I take a very important call from a very important person who does not like to be kept waiting. Are you with me?"

"Yessir."

"And this, Foster, is the situation we find ourselves in. A very important person who does not like to be kept waiting has called. *Now, get Charleena on the phone!*"

"Okay." I knocked on the door again. Mentioned the very important person.

"Tell Stan it's over for me."

"He's not going to like that, Miss Charleena—"

"Tell him!"

I told him.

"I'm not happy right now, Foster. And I like to be happy. It's a green light if we can get Charleena attached. The script is brilliant, the director is rewriting it. It's a huge tent-pole movie that will drive the studio machine. *Tell her that.*"

I have no idea what he just said. I knocked again. "I need to come in!"

"What is it?" she hollered.

"Miss Charleena, Mr. Stan said something about a green machine with a pole and a tent." Dr. Weber stared at me. I walked over to the big canopy bed and handed her the phone. "Please talk to him."

This was some job Macon gave me!

"Stan, darlin', you call at the worst times. . . . I know . . . I know . . . I'm at death's door. . . . *What?* I am most certainly not afraid to get back out there, Stanley! I deeply resent your tone!"

It was good to hear her sounding crabby again. Dr. Weber took Miss Charleena's temperature in her ear while she talked. "Perfectly normal," the doctor muttered.

Miss Charleena shook her head. "It peaks in the afternoon. . . ."

I decided to be confused someplace else. I went back to the kitchen where nothing I could see was attached except the cabinets. There was no green machine and no pole, just brownies. I touched the pan. It had cooled enough. I cut the brownies into squares. I ate one and put the rest on a plate with the chocolate mayonnaise cupcakes.

Dr. Weber came into the kitchen. "Charleena needs to rest. You can go home."

"Is she really dying?"

"I imagine Charleena will outlive us all." He looked at the brownies.

"Do you want one?"

I could tell he did.

"They're warm," I added.

He smiled, took the biggest square, and gobbled it down. "What was your name again?"

"Foster McFee, sir."

Dr. Weber walked out the door. "I'll remember that."

COOK'S TIP: *If you want to be remembered, bake.*

Nineteen

REMEMBER ME?

I poked my head in Angry Wayne's. The counter was full. My baked goods were gone.

"Where you been?" Wayne demanded.

"Around."

He pointed to the empty case.

"You want me to bake more, sir?"

"One dozen delivered here tomorrow morning."

Betty slapped the counter. "Pay the girl, Wayne."

He mumbled something and handed me an envelope. I was in business!

"Mr. Wayne, do you want the chocolate chip muffins and vanilla cupcakes again? Or if you want a change, I could bake butterscotch muffins and the moistest chocolate cupcakes the world has ever seen."

Betty's head shot up. Angry Wayne crossed his arms. "You're the baker. Bring the best you've got."

* * *

I killed myself making these. I got up early and baked them so they'd be perfectly fresh. I used my special striped paper liners, too. When I took them from the oven, the butterscotch smell filled the Bullet, and Sonny's chocolate cupcakes were enough to wake Mama, who normally can sleep through a hurricane.

Mama's nose twitched. "You baked extra?"

"Two dozen."

"Good." She went back to sleep. I piled the frosting on.

"Those smell wonderful." It was Macon. What was he doing here?

"You're sick," I told him.

"Not anymore." I handed him a cupcake. He ate it in two bites. "You should sell these, Foster. I'm not kidding. Could I bring one to Miss Charleena? I can start working for her again."

"Oh." I looked down. "I was there yesterday, and she stayed in her room."

"She doesn't know you that well, Foster. She knows me."

"Well . . ." I said.

So much for learning how to read.

"You can keep the money for the days you worked, but I'll keep ten percent because I got you the work. You know, like a movie agent."

He counted out the money and gave it to me.

"I talked to her agent," I said.

Macon stopped dead at that. "You talked to Stanley Bull?"

"He said his name was Stan."

"You actually spoke to him?"

"Yeah. He wanted to talk to her, and she didn't want to talk to him."

"I've never even answered the phone!"

I shrugged. "It was ringing."

"Stan Bull is one of the biggest agents in Hollywood."

I mentioned how Miss Charleena got angry on the phone and told him she wasn't afraid of getting back out there. "Do you know what that means?"

"It's personal information, Foster."

Elvis the cat crept by. I gave him a dirty look.

"I've got to go back to Miss Charleena's now."

"You want me to go with you? I mean, I think she likes me and—"

"Miss Charleena doesn't really like anyone, Foster."

"I think she likes me. We had a long talk—"

"This is *my* job, Foster. Not yours."

"I know. But maybe I could help her and—"

Macon's eyes got a funny look and his voice changed. "It sounds like you're trying to steal my job!"

What was he talking about?

"It sounds like you got real involved over there, Foster. Real involved!"

"That's crazy, Macon!"

"I'm going to leave now."

"Good!"

Elvis the cat jumped out from behind a bush. Stupid, sneaky cat!

I watched Macon storm off down the driveway.

You want to know a big issue I've got? Being accused of something I didn't do!

Lester walked up. "Just so you know, Charleena Hendley can seem like she's your friend one day and ignore you for months after. Don't let it get to you."

Kind of late for that.

* * *

I dropped the baked goods off at Angry Wayne's and I think I almost saw him smile when I put them in the plastic container.

"How much you charging?" Clay asked.

Wayne thought about that. "Dollar seventy-five."

"Yesterday they were a dollar fifty."

"Hold on to your seats, boys. These are about to be famous."

Yes!

"You add one with my eggs instead of toast?" Clay asked him.

"Nope."

Two men at the counter were wearing green uniforms and mirrored sunglasses. I bet they worked at the prison. "Give me one of each," one of the men said.

"Same," said the other.

Wayne pointed to a plate and said to me, "Give Charlie and Zeke what they asked for."

I put a muffin and a cupcake on two plates and put them in front of the men. Charlie and Zeke ate them fast without saying anything. The biggest man burped, chugged down coffee, pushed the empty plate toward me. "Hit me again."

"Same."

"I want a cupcake," Betty said, and another man said he'd take what was left.

Clay raised his hand. "What about me?"

"He who hesitates is lost," Wayne told him.

"You want me to bring more tomorrow?" I asked.

"Yep."

I decided to leave while I was ahead.

★ ★ ★

The bus was orange, there was no missing that. A lady was standing outside of it saying hi to everybody. Little kids were getting books, and other people were bringing books back. I got close to this lady who was smiling and laughing. She was wearing dangling book earrings.

I saw Garland coming out of the bus. "Hey!" he shouted.

"Hey."

"Mrs. Worth," Garland said, "this is Foster. She's new to town."

"Welcome to the Bookmobile, Foster. What kind of a book can I get you?"

"Uh . . ."

I felt like I had a sign around my neck: THIS GIRL CAN'T READ.

Her book earrings swayed.

"She's a baker," Garland said.

Mrs. Worth patted her stomach. "I'm an eater. I've got all kinds of cookbooks inside. Garland knows where they are."

You don't know how much I'd love to read a cookbook.

"Come on, Foster!" He climbed in the bus.

Okay, but . . .

I followed him. There was a desk with a swivel chair and posters of people holding books, there were tall cases slanted back stuffed with books, and there was Amy sitting on the floor reading. She was wearing shorts and a black shirt with a purple thunderbolt across it.

Garland stepped over her.

She kept reading. "I see you, Garland."

I bent down so she could see my face and waved. Amy said, "Welcome to the inner sanctum, Foster."

I giggled. Garland climbed up a step stool and handed me books—one with chocolate cookies on the cover, one with a beautifully set table, one with a deep-dish blueberry pie. He looked through the stack and handed one down with a strawberry cake on the cover.

Cookbooks are heavy. "These look good," I told him.

"Wait, there's more."

"That's okay, Garland, these are—"

Amy looked up. "Do you guys think having free

coffee and cookies on Saturday will bring people to the store?"

"I thought your dad said you couldn't do that," I mentioned

"Let's assume I can convince him. What do you think?"

"It sounds good," Garland said.

"It depends on the cookies," I added.

Amy was surprised. "It does?"

"Totally."

"I thought Oreos."

I shook my head.

"Chips Ahoy?"

Please.

"Boring won't work," I told her.

"My whole life is boring, Foster! I'm trying to bring new ideas to the hardware store and my dad just looks at me like I'm an alien."

"You are an alien." Garland held up another cookbook. It was big, it was yellow, and it had Sonny Kroll's picture on it.

I couldn't believe it.

"*Sonny Side Up* with Sonny Kroll. You want it?"

I didn't know Sonny had a book! "I want it." I put the

others down. He handed it to me. I held it like it was made of diamonds.

"Come on." He climbed down and stepped over Amy, and we headed outside. "Foster wants this one, Mrs. Worth"

"Good choice. This book just came out. I love that man's show."

She filled out a card for me, and when I told her where I lived, she said, "Address: Silver Bullet behind Kitty and Lester's, Culpepper, West VA, USA."

I grinned. That's an excellent address.

She stamped the book and gave it to me. "You bring it back in three weeks."

I held it over my heart.

Mrs. Worth smiled. "That's where a book should be carried."

Twenty

I HELD TIGHT to Sonny's cookbook as Garland and I walked up a path behind Angry Wayne's. "My mom and I started Helping Hands House a year ago," he told me.

"It's where prisoners' families stay, right?"

"Yeah. They stay for a few days and we try to help them with the expenses." Garland shook his head. "But we're basically broke."

We walked toward a broken-down house. Three women were sitting on the porch steps. A little girl came running up to us.

"Did you bring breakfast?" she asked us.

Garland bent down. "Didn't you get breakfast?"

"No."

One of the women walked up. "We're low on food."

"I want scrambled eggs," the little girl whispered.

Garland's jaw got hard as we walked inside, past

rickety stairs, to the kitchen. He opened the refrigerator. No eggs, no toast. There was some margarine and juice. The little girl followed me. She held up an empty jar. "The grape jelly's gone, too."

I put Sonny's book on top of the refrigerator. "Maybe I can help. I'll be right back, okay?" I ran outside, down the path, and into Angry Wayne's.

The sheriff, Betty, and two other men sat at the counter.

"Heard crime's up by Fish's place."

Mama hadn't told me that!

The sheriff nodded. "Wait till more of 'em get out on parole and have to get jobs around here. We're going to see some changes, boy."

"We're going to see some changes," they all said. Betty took a big gulp of coffee.

Wayne threw a ball at the wall; the buzzer went off. "One a these days I'm going to make a citizen's arrest!"

The sheriff chuckled. "I'd pay to see that."

"If you see it, Boone, you'd better come and help me!"

Here goes. "I need a favor, sir."

Angry Wayne glared at me. He didn't seem to be the kind that did too many favors.

"I need some eggs and bread for Helping Hands.

There's a little girl over there who hasn't had breakfast."

"How crazy are you, girl?"

Pretty crazy.

"Those people are freeloaders—every last one of them."

Betty slapped the counter. "They've got real needs, Wayne. Those families are broke and hurting."

I gulped. "You could just take the money out of what you owe me, sir."

The door opened and Garland walked in.

"You in on this scheme?" Wayne asked him.

Garland stood next to me. Betty leaned across the counter. "Do something for someone, Wayne."

His face got pink. He threw a ball at the buzzer.

Garland whispered, "Let's go, Foster." We headed out the door.

"How many eggs you need?" Wayne asked.

I turned around. "A dozen."

"Two dozen," Garland said.

Wayne walked in the back and came out with two cartons of eggs. He took a loaf of bread down from the shelf. I needed one more thing.

"Thank you so much! Have you got a little grape jelly for this little girl who—"

Betty pointed. "It's behind the counter."

"I know where it is!" Angry Wayne reached down and slammed a jar of grape jelly on the counter. "Now git."

Garland grabbed the jelly. We shouted, "Thank you!" and tore out the door.

★ ★ ★

We ran into Helping Hands. "Okay, we've got breakfast with grape jelly!"

The kids shouted yay and I set to work. Garland plugged in the toaster. I broke eggs into a bowl one-handed like I learned on the Food Network.

"How do you do that?" the little girl asked. She was the cutest thing, with long dark hair and blue eyes.

"You flick your wrist."

"I want to try!"

I pictured eggs all over the floor. "You have to be older."

She flopped down. "You have to be older for everything!"

"Not for grape jelly." I handed it to her. "You put it on the table."

She held up a book. "After breakfast will you read me a story?"

I wished I could. I beat the eggs. "I might have to leave right after."

"I'll read it to you," Garland told her. "What's your name?"

"Delilah May Canning."

"I'm Foster," I said.

"That's a boy's name!"

I added a little salt. "Do I look like a boy?"

"Nope." Garland plugged in the toaster. That got me grinning.

I scrambled eggs. Garland toasted bread. We fed nine people breakfast. I hadn't felt this good in I don't know when.

Delilah May Canning held her book up. "It's time for my story!"

"You read it," I told Garland. I took Sonny's cookbook from the top of the refrigerator and headed home.

* * *

I'd just come out of FOOD when Miss Charleena pulled up in her little blue sports car. She was wearing a hot pink top, white jeans, and long gold earrings, and she was smiling. "Where have you been?"

Was she kidding? "I was at your house, but you were sick."

"Oh, that," she said. "It comes and goes. I thought you'd be coming by so we could talk about reading."

My heart fluttered at that, but then I remembered Lester saying she could be friendly one minute and then ignore you for months.

"What book do you have there, Foster?"

I showed her Sonny's cookbook. She leafed through it. "Maple pecan cupcakes with maple frosting. My, that sounds dangerous."

I looked over at the page she was reading. I want to make that!

"Miss Charleena, here's what you've got to know. Reading's a serious thing with me. I want to do it, and I'm scared to try." This next part was harder. "But if it's not a serious thing with you—I mean, if you'd just lose interest after a while—I'm not saying you would, but just in case . . . then, I don't think we should do it."

She closed the book with a snap and handed it back to me.

I wanted to evaporate like spit on a hot road. "I shouldn't have said that, Miss Charleena. I'm sorry."

"Foster, I *do* want to talk with you about reading."

That sounded like she meant it. "Miss Charleena, I want to read Sonny's book. Can you teach me?"

"This is too hard to start with—"

"No! This is the one I want to read!"

"I understand, but—"

"No, ma'am, you don't understand. This book's got my name on it!"

"Well then, Foster McFee, we'll give it a try."

I'd better warn her. "I've got to tell you something else, Miss Charleena. I've tried reading before. I tried with everything I had, and my brain closes up."

She nodded. "My teacher told me some people come naturally to reading and others have to work twice as hard. There's nothing wrong with having a different way of learning. What's wrong is when people blame you for it."

Miss Charleena, you don't know what you just said to me.

"Come by tomorrow and bring your book. But not too early. I need my beauty sleep."

And with that, she sped away.

Twenty-One

I SAUTÉED RED peppers and red onions, added ground beef, and sautéed that, too. "I don't know if anyone can teach me to read, Mama." I'd told her all that happened with Miss Charleena.

"I admire how you're open to the process even though it's been hard," she said.

"It's been impossible." I added tomato paste to the pot, salt, pepper, chili powder, and a little cinnamon.

Mama smiled. "What I can tell you, Baby, is you've got grit, smarts, courage, and heart."

I stirred a pinch of sugar into the chili. "I'm kind of scared to try again, Mama."

"That's natural. Just take the next step and don't look too far down the road." She looked over her reading glasses at me. "I know what you've got inside."

* * *

I woke up at 5:30 A.M., which I figured was way too early to head over to Miss Charleena's, but I can tell you, every part of me was awake!

I got up, washed, and got dressed without waking Mama. I stood by the sink, looking at Lester's daddy's stupid, dead fish.

I said, "I want you to know that I'm going to do something important today. More important than a fish could understand. I don't know why I'm telling you, except that I want to say it out loud, so here goes. Today, I'm going to start learning to read!"

I pretended the fish wiggled his fishtail like a dog.

"I know it's going to be hard, so I'm getting ready for that, but I just feel this time I'm not going to get caught up in all the things that have held me back. I guess you know about getting caught, don't you?"

I stood there for a minute.

"All right then. I'm going."

* * *

I delivered the butterscotch muffins and chocolate cupcakes to Angry Wayne, and he handed me an envelope with money in it.

"Mr. Wayne, you were supposed to keep this money so I could pay you back for the food you gave me for Helping Hands."

"Take the money," he said.

"But sir—"

Betty sipped her coffee. "Don't mess with the miracle, Foster."

I was hoping to see another miracle at Miss Charleena's, but when I got there Macon opened the door.

"Oh," I said. "Hi."

"What do you want?"

"Miss Charleena and I have an appointment."

"What about?"

"About . . . *stuff* . . ." I decided to be mature. "How's your movie coming?"

"It's not."

"How come?"

You'd have thought I'd asked him to jump off a building. "*It's just not, okay?*"

Okay.

"She's watching TV." He walked away.

I went into the room off the kitchen. Miss Charleena was sitting on a big couch watching a wide-screen TV. A lady in a long skirt was talking to a group of kids not in America. Then I realized, that wasn't just any lady, that was Miss Charleena. She was much younger than she is now, but still!

"This is my big scene," Miss Charleena said. "I played a teacher in India." I sat down and watched as the lady, I mean Miss Charleena, looked at the kids and said, "Boys and girls, I want to tell you a story. One day a businessman was traveling in India, and he happened to see a huge elephant standing there with his front foot chained to a small fence. The businessman knew the elephant had the strength to yank that fence down, so he asked the trainer why the elephant stood there like it couldn't move. 'Ah,' said the trainer, 'this is how you train an elephant. From the time he was a baby we had that chain around his front foot. He tried to break free when he was little, but couldn't do it. By the time he had grown, he'd stopped trying. That great elephant didn't know his own strength.'"

Miss Charleena as the teacher looked at the children. "That happens to all of us from time to time. I believe it is time for you to realize your strength and use it."

The kids looked at each other, and one by one they began to stand.

My heart was pounding. I stood, too.

★ ★ ★

"Yank, darlin'." Miss Charleena pointed to a big word in Sonny's cookbook.

Appetizers.

I made a face. "It's a great word," she explained. "Look." She wrote out *app e tiz ers.* "Can you sound some of it out?"

I put my hand over the *app.* "App," I said. I put my finger on the *e.* "E." I got through the *tiz* and the *er* after some work.

"And see, this word comes from other words you know. *Appetite, appetizing.* So, the next time you see it, it can be a clue." Miss Charleena tapped the book. "We've got a world of recipes here."

She opened the book to a page. "Can you sound that out?"

I looked at it.

Banana Cake with Fudge Frosting.

"We're starting pretty fast," I mentioned.

She wrote out *ba na na.* "Another great word. It's written exactly as it sounds."

Slowly, I sounded it out and Miss Charleena handed me an actual banana.

"But the word *cake* has a tricky letter," she told me.

"*C* can sound like a *k* as in *cake*, or it can sound like an *s* as in *cereal*."

"Why did they do that?"

"There are rules for cooking; there are rules for letters and words."

"Always preheat the oven," I said. "Make sure the butter is softened before you cream it."

"You've probably learned dozens of cooking rules. You're already good at learning rules."

I never thought of it that way.

★ ★ ★

But, after an hour, my brain was close to busting. Twice I shouted, "I can't get it! It's too hard!" But not once did I run out of the room. Not once did I feel embarrassed, because Miss Charleena kept saying, "Take your time. Do this at your speed."

When we got to the end of the banana cake recipe, I was so sick of it, I didn't want to make this cake at all. But slowly I could sound out "mash the banana with a fork" on my own, because not one of those words was tricky. People should spend more time using nontricky words, in my opinion. Miss Charleena even handed me a fork and I mashed a banana on her counter and thought about what the words looked like in Sonny's cookbook. I'd love to turn this recipe into cupcakes.

I heard a noise and looked up. Macon was standing at the kitchen door.

I'd forgotten he was in the house.

"I didn't mean to interrupt," he began.

I felt my face turn red. He'd probably been standing there forever, thinking how dumb I am mashing a banana with a fork and saying it out loud.

Now he knew I couldn't read.

He'd probably tell everybody!

Like Daddy learned in the army, I could stay and fight or leave without too many casualties. "I've gotta go," I said, and headed toward the door.

"Foster," Miss Charleena said, "wait!"

Reading had caused me enough wounds. I was outta here.

"Foster!"

I ran past Macon, not looking at him. He was laughing at me, probably, thinking I was stupid.

I ran out the back door and raced down the hill. I heard the awful siren blaring from the prison. I was in my own kind of jail where the gates lock tight, and no matter what, you just can't get out.

Twenty-Two

I WAS BREATHING hard when I got to the main road. I was remembering, too, all the way back to first grade when I got put in the lowest reading group, the Daisies. Some kids called us the Dandelions.

"Dandelions, dumb dandelions," they'd shout.

I ran toward Fish Hardware, remembering the guy who worked at the ice cream place in Nashville, who sneered at me when I said I wanted chocolate. He pointed to a big board. "What kind of chocolate?" I didn't know, I didn't care, I just wanted to get out of there. So I ran off, just like now.

"If you applied yourself, Foster . . ." Mrs. Ritter always told me.

I only knew about applying glue to something to make it stick. Applying myself to school seemed like school would stick all over me and never come off.

"What in the world are we going to do with you?" Mrs. Ritter asked.

I could think of a few things.

Take it easy on me.

Teach me different.

Care about me just a little.

So many times that year I wanted to shout, "It's not like I'm waking up in the morning and trying to mess up. I just don't get it!"

And now Macon knew.

I got to Fish Hardware. Mama always said if I was ever in need she'd drop everything.

I walked inside past brooms and hammers and lightbulbs and tools of every kind. I walked past Amy.

"Hi, Foster."

I didn't say hi back.

"Are you okay?"

I shook my head. I heard Mama's voice coming from the back.

"If I were you, I'd paint it a deep blue and use this bright white paint on the windows and ceiling. That room will pop like you can't believe!"

I walked over to where Mama was talking to a big woman who had her back to me. "Hi there," Mama said to me.

I started crying. I didn't mean to, honest.

"Baby, what's wrong?"

Amy headed over. The big woman turned around. It was that principal, Mrs. Dupree!

That made me cry harder.

"Foster," Mama said. "What happened?"

Mrs. Dupree stared at me, waiting for my answer.

"We can't live in this town anymore!" I shouted. "We can't!"

* * *

I pulled the sheet around my bed. It wasn't much of a place to hide. I felt like I did when I was little, throwing a sheet over a table and sitting underneath it. I needed a fort where nobody could reach me. Normally when I'd get upset, I'd hug Daddy's pillowcase and it would make me feel a little better.

All I had was a sleeping pillowcase with nothing special inside. I threw it on the floor.

I hated Huck!

"Foster." It was Mama. "Someone's here to see you."

"I can't see anyone right now."

I heard a girl's voice say, "I'll just leave them here, Mrs. McFee."

I dried my face on my shirt and pushed the curtain back. Amy was standing there holding the prettiest flowers. "I thought these might make you feel better, Foster."

"That's so nice. I'm sorry I ran out."

"Everybody has bad days." She looked around the Bullet. "This is so cool. You have your own inner sanctum."

Amy and I had a chocolate cupcake, and it didn't take long before I told her I wanted to be the first kid on the Food Network.

"The way I've got it figured, the cooking world needs a famous kid chef who isn't afraid to stir things up. That's a cooking joke."

She laughed. "I can see you doing that, Foster! I've got a dream, too, but it's dumb."

"Dreams aren't dumb."

"Well," she whispered. "I want to be a singer."

I told her about Mama.

"I've heard her singing to herself, Foster, and I thought, she's so good!"

"You should talk to her about it."

"I couldn't . . . I mean, I could. I'm brave about hardware, but singing is so personal."

She needed some coaching. "Look, you can't wait for people to come to you. You've got to get out there and make your own breaks."

She looked down nervously.

"I've been at this awhile. It takes time."

I told her about my NEVER, NEVER, NEVER GIVE UP sign that I had back in Memphis. I didn't mention that I tore it up in sixth grade after Johnny Joe Badger called me the "stupidest girl in Memphis." There were some pretty stupid girls in that town.

I told her how Eddington Carver and I were watching this ant crawling around trying to carry something twice his size. The ant kept dropping it, but he picked it back up again and again. Eddington counted seventeen times.

"You've got to be like an ant," I told her.

I told her how it took years for Sonny Kroll to become a famous chef. "Nobody wanted him at first. He wrote letters, he knocked on doors, he made DVDs. Finally, he got a break. And you know what he said? He appreciated it all the more because it didn't come easy."

I figured that was enough for one day. I also figured I should probably take my own advice.

★ ★ ★

Mama, Kitty, and Lester were standing outside the Bullet as Amy left. Something didn't feel right. As Amy headed down the road, Mama said, "Lester heard something on the news, Baby."

"What?"

Lester put his hands in his pockets and sighed. "Well, this cook you love so much, Sonny Kroll. I'm sorry to tell you, but it seems like he was in a bad accident."

I felt a bolt go through me.

"He got knocked off his motorcycle, and he's in the hospital. He's in critical care."

"No!"

"He's in a hospital in California," Lester added.

"He's not going to die!"

"Honey, I don't know. They said on the news he's in a coma."

"People can get better from that, right?"

Lester nodded. "Sometimes."

"But sometimes means yes, right?"

Tears ran down my face.

Don't die on me, Sonny. Don't die.

⋆ ⋆ ⋆

It was late. I couldn't sleep. Sonny always wore a helmet when he rode that bike. I pictured him lying by the side of the road.

I can't just lie here.

I went to the kitchen quietly and looked at his cookbook. I got a piece of paper and a pen. The clock read 11:38 P.M. How come I could read a clock and not a book? How come I could write my name and not a letter?

This is what I wanted to write:

Dear Sonny,

I never wanted to be good at writing the way I do now. If I was good, I'd write you a poem about all you've given me. You've brought so many ingredients into my life. You've taught me to be brave and to always share what I've got with other people. You're not just a cook, you're my friend, and I want you to know I'm cheering for you here in West Virginia to get better. I want you to know that I'm only twelve, but I've been watching your show for five years, since my daddy died. I want you to know that I think you're close to the best man I know.

Your #1 Fan,
Foster McFee, soon to be seen on Cooking with Foster

But I didn't know how to write all that down. Slowly, I wrote what I could:

Deer Sonny

U R not a loan.

Twenty-Three

I WALKED UP to Miss Charleena's back door carrying the cookbook. I didn't care who answered. I didn't care if Macon had told the whole world that I couldn't read. I was going to read this cookbook if it killed me.

Macon was watering the flowers. I didn't look at him. I knocked. Miss Charleena answered. I held Sonny's cookbook out to her. I told her about his accident.

"I'm ready to do this now," I told her. "I'm not going to run away."

* * *

I wanted to take those words back any number of times, but I didn't. Sometimes it took three days to get through one recipe. Once I tried to teach Miss Charleena how to make butterscotch brownies, and she kept saying, "How do I know if I've overmixed the batter?"

"Well, you just know. . . ."

"How do I know if the muffin springs back when I touch it? How much does it spring back?"

"Well . . ."

She was worse at cooking than I was at reading.

Once I just slammed Sonny's cookbook shut and started crying.

"Foster," she said. "Maybe I'm the wrong person to help you. I'm not a teacher!"

"I think you're doing really well." A guy said it.

I turned around. It was Macon.

What's it to you?

"I think it's cool you're doing this." He looked up at me smiling. "I know what it's like to have to deal with something that's always a problem. The problem with my problem is that everyone can see it and it can't be fixed."

"What's your problem?"

"I'm short!" He stood there, small and miserable.

"You're not that short," I lied.

"Last year the teacher called me to read something in class. She said, 'Stand up, Macon,' and I did. Then she shouted, 'I said, stand up, young man!' And I was already standing! All the kids were laughing."

I bit my lip so I wouldn't smile.

"People call me names like elf and pipsqueak. A documentary filmmaker called pipsqueak? And there's squirt, shrimp, small-fry, dinky, and"—he shuddered—"*mini Macon*. It kills me, Foster. I feel tall inside."

I smiled. "People call me stupid, dumbo, and dunce."

"You're none of those things. You're smart."

"Thanks." I wish I could tell him he wasn't little.

"You need to know something about me, Foster. I would never call you a name or make fun of you. So, look. I'm a good reader and I could help you. And if you want to help me, I still need an assistant. You don't have to take notes. You can help me think of questions to ask the people who work at the prison."

"You mean, like, 'Have you ever had problems with a prisoner?'"

"Yes, exactly." Macon was writing.

"Have you ever wondered how the prisoners feel about you?"

"That's excellent."

"Do you ever feel sorry for them?"

"Yes!"

"But I think to really learn about the prison, you've got to go to the Helping Hands House, Macon."

"I hadn't thought about that." He wrote that down,

too. I'd never had anybody take notes when *I* was talking. "I can't believe anyone would ever think you were stupid."

The widest smile took over my face.

Macon, you have no idea what you just said to me.

★ ★ ★

Those next weeks weren't easy, I'll tell you, because three people had made it their business to teach me how to read. I'd made it my business, too, but Miss Charleena, Mama, and Macon were on my case day and night.

Macon wrote my job out on paper:

ASSISTANT

"This is what you are," he said. "Let's sound it out."

"Ass . . ." I began. "Hey, wait a minute!"

"It's phonics, Foster!"

Mama arranged things from Fish Hardware on the table, then she wrote the name of each thing on a sticky note. HAMMER, NAIL, CURTAIN ROD, PAINTBRUSH, PLUNGER. She said it might help if I could see the thing and the word that went with it. After the lesson, the toilet overflowed. Mama grabbed the plunger and started pumping.

"Plunger," I said. "P-l-u-n—"

"Foster, just grab some towels right now!"

After I cleaned up, I asked Mama to write out, *She grabbed the towels and cleaned up the mess.* It helped to see the thing I'd just done written out, and I used my amazing memory to memorize what the words looked like.

"Do you think memorizing is cheating in reading?" I asked Mama.

"You use whatever God's given you, Baby."

I felt like yeast was in my brain and it was rising. Sometimes I'd stand in front of the bathroom mirror and look to see if my head had doubled.

Sometimes I had to tell people, *Enough! My brain can't take anymore.* But it was better to be surrounded by people who were trying too hard than by people who didn't care. Kitty wanted to help, too.

"You know what killed me in school?" she groaned. "Word problems in math."

"Those are the worst!" I agreed.

She laughed. "Donny has six cats and Susie has nine. If Susie gives three cats to Donny . . ." She shook her head laughing.

I finished it for her. "And then five more cats show up on Donny's porch so he has to give two back to Susie, how many cats does Donny have?"

We looked at each other and shouted, "Too many!"

I put a big sign with the alphabet right under Lester's daddy's stupid, dead fish. I taped paper underneath it and wrote down the new words I was learning. This way, when I was cooking, I could have reading right in my face.

Every night before bed I said to the fish, "Guard these words and letters. I'm counting on you."

Twenty-Four

YOU KNOW HOW it is when you're learning something hard? You have a breakthrough and then you take twelve steps backward and forget you learned anything.

One day I'd feel my brain open up; the next day it would be locked tight. Miss Charleena never seemed frustrated with me. I guess I was frustrated enough for both of us.

Sonny's show was in reruns, and all anyone said was he was in critical condition. I renewed his cookbook at the Bookmobile. Then, to honor him, I turned his banana cake with fudge frosting into amazing cupcakes.

"I can move two dozen cupcakes a day if you're up to it," Wayne told me.

I was! I baked red velvet cupcakes with fluffy white frosting; I made apple cupcakes with caramel frosting.

I sure liked having a little baking business. I was even getting stopped on the street.

Where did you learn to bake like that?

When are you going to make the chocolate ones again?

Those lemon cupcakes were dry.

That last one hurt. "I fell asleep waiting for them to bake," I explained to the man who said my lemon cupcakes were dry.

He climbed into his pickup and told me, "If you're going to put yourself out there, be ready to take your fouls."

"You can't make everybody happy," Mama told me later.

Then Amy had an idea. "A new cupcake, Foster. A cupcake no one has ever eaten in Culpepper. I want you to make it, and we're going to give them out on the first Cool Tool Saturday. Daddy said we could try this. I want to go all out."

I smiled. "How about chocolate malt?"

She sat down. "This is possible?"

In the cupcake world, anything is possible.

And on Saturday I brought thirty-six chocolate malt cupcakes to Fish Hardware, and Amy gave me thirty-six dollars—which was very cool. Mama arranged them on a plate; the coffee was waiting. A swarm of people came into the store.

Amy held up "the ultimate cool tool, a must-have for anyone interested in anything." Angry Wayne, Kitty, Lester, the sheriff, and Betty were watching as she took it out of a leather case and began to unfold it. "This," she said proudly, "is the Über Tool. It's got a hammer, screwdriver, bottle opener, flashlight, wrench, first aid kit, pliers, scissors, nail file, wire, and a personal cooling device." A little fan whirred.

Angry Wayne ate two of my chocolate malt cupcakes and bought the first Über Tool. He turned to me. "Why haven't we sold these cupcakes at my restaurant?"

"Amy wanted something brand-new, sir."

"I want these cupcakes at my place Monday morning," he ordered.

Amy marched over. "These are hardware cupcakes."

Angry Wayne stared her down. "These cupcakes belong to the world."

★ ★ ★

"My dad would have liked the Über Tool, Foster. He was always fixing something." Garland smiled. We were outside Fish Hardware. "He fixed my running."

"How did he do that?"

"I was fast, but I didn't want to practice. And one day I ran a really bad race. I didn't even finish. I made my school lose. And he told me, 'Look, sport, it's a gift to be fast, and it's your job to see how far you can go with it.' He told me, when you start a race, you've got to finish it. And you know the crazy part? He had one leg a little shorter than the other, so he couldn't run. . . ." Garland gulped and looked away.

"He sounds awesome."

"I've never had a coach so good. I try to go back over everything he told me."

I know exactly what he meant.

Amy came outside grinning. "The cupcakes are gone, Foster. And we sold *thirteen* Über Tools. I think we've hit the tipping point!"

★ ★ ★

There was energy popping in the air. It felt like Culpepper was waking up. Macon finished an apple cupcake with caramel frosting, his favorite, and said, "Okay, you guys. It's time."

Garland and I nodded.

"It's time to do what we have to do."

"*You* have to do it," Garland reminded him.

Macon stood by the Culpepper prison gate and

announced to the guard, "I am a documentary filmmaker. I'm making a movie about how this prison has affected Culpepper. I'd like to speak to the warden."

Macon had been practicing this line all day, but he needed to grow another foot to be taken seriously. The guard looked at him. "Very funny."

"It's not funny!" Macon insisted. "This is serious!"

Garland and I looked serious. I should have brought cupcakes.

"This prison has made promises to this town that it hasn't fulfilled!" Macon insisted.

"Step away from the gate," the guard said.

Macon had memorized this next part, too. "I'm making this request as a citizen of Culpepper."

The guard laughed. "How old are you?"

"Almost thirteen!"

"Step away from the gate, junior."

Garland and I dragged Macon off, which was harder than you'd think. He was little, but all his issues had risen to the top.

"You've lied to this town!" Macon screamed.

"I just work here, little man. Get lost!"

"That's what we're doing, sir." We dragged Macon down the road.

"I'm never going to get my movie made!"

Garland lifted him over a pothole. "I think it's good to practice and all, but maybe you should wait until you get your camera."

"I want to film the big stories, you guys, and show people all the ways we're being lied to." He looked miserable as a prison bus drove by.

"I think you're the perfect one to do that," I told him.

He looked up hopefully. "You do?"

"It's like you're angry for all of us."

His face changed to all-out happiness. "That's exactly what a doc filmmaker does, Foster. Be angry for the world. You're a genius!" His face was red. "I have to hold on to my anger."

"I don't think that's going to be a problem, Macon."

★ ★ ★

Lots of people in town were angry. The word was that Taco Terrific had offered Mr. Fish a lot of money for the church and he was going to sell it. Every time Perseverance Wilson saw Mr. Fish, she hollered he was "messing with sacred ground."

Angry Wayne wore a shirt that had a taco with an X through it.

I wore a shirt with a cupcake on it, but that didn't mean I wasn't mad.

And then Mama dropped her bomb.

I was mashing bananas for banana cupcake batter when she did it. She walked through the door; the smile was out of her eyes.

"What's wrong?" I asked.

"Nothing." She started cleaning up around the Bullet—wiping things down that looked clean to me. Mama does that when something's wrong.

"You still have the job at Fish Hardware?"

"Of course."

"You feeling sick or something?"

"No."

She didn't say much at dinner. She didn't say much as we were doing the dishes. We went outside and sat in the fold-up chairs. The strange glow from the prison filled the night sky.

"I've got to go away for a few days," she said.

I didn't like the sound of that. "Where are you going?"

She looked at her hands. "Back to Memphis. I've got to take care of a few things."

Memphis! "I'll come with you."

She took my hand. "You need to stay here with Kitty and Lester. They said it's okay. I'll only be gone for a couple of days."

My mouth felt dry all of a sudden. "What have you got to do?"

"Well, we left pretty quick, you know. And there's the bank and some forms I've got to fill out."

There's Huck, I thought. "You think going alone is a good idea, Mama?"

She looked up at the hard glow in the sky. "I need to do this myself."

* * *

I didn't sleep too well. I kept tossing and turning and thinking about Mama driving alone. I thought about her seeing Huck and got a sick feeling. The more I thought about it, the sicker I felt.

When Mama put her suitcase in the car that morning, I handed her the good lunch I'd packed. "You're strong, Mama, and you're a fighter. Remember that." I hugged her with a lot more courage than I had.

She got in the Chevy smiling brave. I watched her pull away and felt like I was getting left. There was nothing in my life that said Mama would up and leave me—I just felt a place of fear open up in my heart. She blew me a big kiss and honked as she drove off. I ran behind the car waving and shouting, "See you Sunday," just in case she forgot.

I walked slowly to Kitty and Lester's house. It didn't seem as friendly as before. Nothing did. I figured if I didn't go up their steps, this whole thing didn't actually start.

I worried about fog rolling in and Mama being in the car by herself. I worried she'd run out of gas, or get lost again, or drive off a cliff. I checked my watch. Exactly three minutes had passed. By the time Sunday came, I was going to be a wreck.

Twenty-Five

MACON AND I were walking to the Bookmobile. I had to turn in Sonny's cookbook.

"I'm really glad you moved here, Foster."

"Thanks."

"How come you did?"

That was a loaded question.

"I've lived here half my life," Macon said. "I came because my daddy ran off. Me and my mom moved in with my grandma."

I waited for him to say more, but he didn't.

"Do you remember your dad?"

"Yes." Macon's face looked hard, like he didn't have any good memories.

"Mama and I had to leave kind of fast," I began.

"What happened?"

I told him a little about Huck, but just a little. "He wasn't the kind of person we should have in our lives," was how I put it.

"My dad wasn't either."

And there passed between us this kind of knowing. We didn't need to talk about it anymore. We walked up the gravel road.

"In addition to my reading stuff, I've got a fear of Elvises."

He stopped and looked up at me, but he wasn't smirking or anything.

"I know it's unnatural," I added.

"My uncle Chester is afraid of Democrats," he said. "He starts shaking all over when he sees one."

We kept walking, heading down the road, hearing the crunch of our shoes on the little stones. I got in step with him, swinging my arms like he was doing, setting my jaw.

I felt safe around this small, determined boy who didn't make fun of anything I told him.

This is how best friends are made.

* * *

I turned in Sonny's book, and Mrs. Worth said, "What can we get you now?"

I didn't want anything else, but Macon said, "Do you have any books on Elvis?"

Had he been listening at all?

Mrs. Worth did a little dance behind her desk and led us to the back section. "Mr. Elvis Presley with photographs," she said, and handed the book to Macon.

Some friend.

Macon sat on the floor and opened the book. "I've been thinking, Foster, about how we need to face our fears."

This was my fear, not his!

"You need to look at this," Macon said. He opened the book to a two-page picture of Elvis in a shirt that looked like it had jewels on it, sweat dripping from his face.

"Macon, stop it! I don't want to think about Elvis."

"But the thing is, Foster, Elvis is hard to avoid. He was so famous, there's probably no place you could go where there isn't a picture of him someplace. You're going to have to deal with it."

I shook my head.

"It's hard in the beginning, but then it gets easier. Here's a picture of Elvis when he was just a boy."

I looked.

"And here's another one when he had a famous TV moment on the *Ed Sullivan Show* long before we were born. See, it's just Elvis from the waist up."

I looked a little longer at that one.

"You're doing fine," Macon said.

I crossed my arms tight. "Huck made me call him Elvis when Mama wasn't around. It was weird. His voice would get low and he'd say he was the real Elvis come back from the dead."

Macon thought about that. "Did Huck have big crowds around him when he sang?"

"Not really."

"Then I can absolutely say, Foster, that Huck was lying. If Elvis had come back from the dead, the crowds would have been huge."

I laughed. "I hadn't thought about that."

"Here's something you should read about how much Elvis loved his mother." Macon showed me the page.

"When Elvis was a boy he told his mother that someday he was going to buy her a fine house."

I hated long sentences.

"I bet real soon you'll be reading paragraphs," he told me.

"Short ones," I said.

* * *

Mama had been gone for three days. I'd talked to her twice, but both times her voice sounded strained. There was no book that would help me get over my fear that she might go back to Huck.

My stomach hurt. I was sitting out in the blue chair when Lester walked up wearing a hat with hooks in it. He was carrying two long fishing poles.

"You ever catch a bass?" he asked me.

"No sir."

He handed me a pole. "I think you're tough enough to do it."

* * *

We walked down the road to a lake that was hidden back in the woods.

Lester sat down on the grass. "I love this place. I don't have to go far to find a fish. My daddy fished here until the day he died."

I thought of the dead fish over the sink and how Lester's daddy had dropped dead in the kitchen.

Lester looked at the lake. "They're biting today."

I didn't see anything biting.

"They know we're here," Lester whispered, "and we're just going to sneak up on them."

Lester put a worm on his hook and one on mine. "Now the thing about fishing is this—if you forget everything else today, remember, you're a whole lot smarter than the fish."

I laughed and thought that would look good on a T-shirt. Maybe I could get one made for the first day of school. I watched him toss his line into the water. I tried to copy him, but my line didn't get too far out in the lake.

"Now we wait," he said.

That didn't seem too exciting. "How long do we wait?"

"Till we get a nibble." He smiled. "When I was in the army sometimes I'd picture this lake back home and see myself right here with a fishing pole."

This little lake sure was pretty. There were rocks along the bank and wildflowers growing.

"When you're going through a tough spell, it's easy to think that's all your life is about. You forget the good things, forget the quiet places. But they're always inside of us and we can pull them up when we need to set ourselves right. I think that's why my pop fished. It just set him right."

I looked at the lake and felt a little guilty that I

was trying to fool a fish that wasn't bothering anybody. Lester got a snap on his line. He yanked his pole, reeled it tighter, and up came one ugly fish.

"Well, Horace," Lester said, "we meet again." He laughed and held the fish up so I could see it. It was not happy about getting caught and made a real fuss on that line. Lester took the hook out of its mouth. "I'm going to send him back in the lake to get ready for our next meeting." He tossed the fish back in. "See you next time, Horace."

"You call the fish Horace?"

"My pop called all basses Horace."

"Why?"

Lester put another worm on his line. "Why not?"

"Excuse me, Lester, but how come you threw the fish back in?"

He laughed. "It makes him smarter."

I sat there waiting for something to happen. You can wait a long time when you're dealing with a smart fish. Lester caught Horace two more times. My line didn't get tight once, but there were other parts to fishing. I felt the sun on my head, heard the birds chirp, and sat next to Lester, peaceful as anything.

"Waiting," he told me, "is a powerful thing. Most

folks today just rush off to get something done. You learn to wait, my young friend. You learn to wait and listen and not be afraid of the quiet. Too much noise in this old world. On a battlefield when you're getting shot at, you don't have time to think things through. You've just got to do as you've been trained and follow your best instincts. It's here in the quiet waiting for a fish that you can fill up for when the tough times come."

I knew I'd heard something important. I wondered if he'd taken me fishing to tell me that.

* * *

"Do you know much about the Iraq War?" I asked him. We headed back up the road carrying our fishing poles.

He looked down at me. "I wasn't in that war, but I've followed it."

"I was wondering what it was like for my daddy. We only got a couple of letters from him and he mostly talked about playing baseball, not fighting."

"There's lots of different situations that he could have been in, Foster."

"He was brave," I told him, "and he was real responsible."

"That's a fine combination for a soldier. I was always looking for people who could fill that bill. I imagine his team counted on him a lot. If I were his CO, I'd a had him be a help to some of the men who weren't as brave, so he could encourage them."

Daddy was one of those go-to people. He'd have people coming out of the woodwork trying to find him when things got tough because he always knew what to do. "I could see him doing that."

"Yeah." Lester squinted in the sun. "Keeping your cool and doing your job the best you can goes a long way in the army. A mighty long way. I imagine your daddy was a hero lots of times, more than you could count."

I smiled.

"I knew a man like your dad. He always had a good word for people, he always gave a pat on the back, he'd carry a wounded friend out of harm's way. Every day he made a difference."

"I bet my daddy did that."

"I bet he did, too. I know the ache of not having him with you, but I hope you can fill that hurt with pride in how he did his job."

I grinned. "Yessir. I can."

Broken places need something to fill them in. I just kept walking with Lester, filling myself up with all he had to say.

When we turned up the road past the broken fence, I saw the Chevy parked in front of the Bullet.

"Your mama made good time," Lester said.

I ran carrying the fishing pole. Mama was out back hanging up wet clothes on the clothesline. She burst into a tired smile when she saw me. I put the pole down and hugged her with everything I had.

"I missed you!" I shouted. "But I did real good."

"I missed you, too, Baby."

I was holding on to her arm when she said, "That arm's a little sore." And she pulled it away. It had a big bruise on it—black and blue.

"What happened?"

"I fell down," she said softly.

"You need a bandage?"

"No." She went back to hanging up her clothes. I felt the tightness go over my chest. I grabbed some clothespins and helped her. I carried the clothes basket into the house, saluted Lester's daddy's dead fish, and flopped on my little bed tucked under the nose of the Bullet.

That's when I saw it. The pillowcase, that is.

Not just any pillowcase, Daddy's Las Vegas pillowcase! I hugged it to my heart. "Mama!" I unzipped it and took out the plastic bag that had all of Daddy's stuff—his dog tags from the army, his letters, his container of mints, his donkey key ring, his little flag of Ireland.

And then it hit me. Mama saw Huck. That's how she got it!

Mama walked inside the Bullet smiling.

"You saw him."

"Just for a little bit. It wasn't right for him to have your daddy's things."

I looked at the bruise on her arm. Mama put her hand over it like she was trying to hide it.

"Did Huck do that?" I asked.

"I told you I fell."

I know what you told me.

Twenty-Six

I TRIED TO talk to Mama over the next few days about how seeing Huck was a bad idea. All I got from her was, "He's not going to bother us anymore. I took care of it."

Then how come he started calling?

"Is this my little Foster child?" he asked when I answered Mama's phone. "Now you know who this is."

I sure did, which was why I hung up.

Another call. "Now, where exactly are you living in West Virginia? I got a cousin up there and I've been meaning to pay him a visit."

I hung up again, and when Mama came home, I let her have it.

"How come you told Huck where we were?"

"Foster, I didn't tell him. I had some papers from Fish Hardware in the car and he saw them."

"He knows we're in Culpepper?"

"I'm not sure about that."

"You said he wasn't going to bother us anymore."

"And I meant what I said!"

This wasn't like Mama. I had a nightmare that an army of Elvises surrounded the Bullet singing his greatest hits. They lifted the trailer up with me and Mama in it and carried us back to Memphis.

★ ★ ★

"What is the matter with you?" Mama demanded.

"Nothing." I looked at the Las Vegas pillowcase with the palm tree and the slot machine and just ached for Daddy. I know Mama went back to get it for me because she loved me, but how could it be worth it if she had to see Huck?

"How did you fall?" I asked her again.

She was folding clothes and didn't look up.

"How did you fall and hurt your arm, Mama?"

"Oh, you know, I was walking down the street and tripped over something and fell facedown."

Mama was wearing shorts and a shirt without sleeves. I didn't see any marks that looked like she'd fallen facedown. "How come you don't have any scratches?" I asked.

"I guess I fell easily."

I can't tell you how much I wanted to shout, "You're lying!" But I didn't.

"You're lucky," I told her.

"Yeah," she said. "Lucky me."

The only other time I remember Mama lying to me was when she came back from parents' night and told me that Mrs. Ritter said I had potential.

I needed fresh air.

I needed to figure out what to do.

I walked right to the Church of God FOR SALE. Perseverance Wilson had planted some pretty red flowers around the steps.

"Come sit with me, Foster."

I headed over. She took a thermos and two cups out of her bag.

"You like iced tea?"

"Yes, ma'am."

She poured me a glass. I took a sip. "That's good."

"I flavor it with a little lemonade. Have a cookie." She took out a tin and opened it.

I grabbed one. This was good, too.

"My mother's lemon icebox cookies. You take as many as you want."

I grabbed two more. "The garden's looking nice," I told her.

"It's getting there." She studied my face. "You don't seem like yourself, if you don't mind me saying."

"I've got lots I'm thinking about." Mama. Sonny. My whole life, actually.

"This is a good place to come and lay your burdens down."

I looked at the boarded-up windows and the locked door and the cracked steps and the big pothole in the little parking lot. It seemed to me this place had its own burdens and couldn't take any more.

"I know what you're thinking," she said.

I sat up straighter. I hoped she couldn't read my mind.

"You're thinking what's the use? Why does that Perseverance Wilson keep holding on to this crumbling building? Why doesn't she just give up and let it go? She can't change anything."

I wasn't thinking that at this moment, but it had occurred to me at other times.

She leaned back smiling. "Oh, I've heard it all before. Let it go, woman. There isn't any money—your pastor up and quit. This church is dead. People have moved on and tacos are moving in." She looked at the boarded-up door.

"But all I see when I look at this old place is the door wide open, fresh paint everywhere, and people singing."

I looked at the church again. I sure couldn't see that.

"I know it's a mess, Foster, but I've got faith."

I looked at her sitting there in her big hat with her blue skirt flowing out over the steps.

"And when I think of Helping Hands, I picture curtains on every window, those rickety steps repaired, and food in the refrigerator."

"I think that's wonderful," I told her. "I'd like to be able to look at a messed-up thing and see something different."

"My daddy was a church janitor all his life, and every day he had something big to clean up. He didn't focus on the mess, he'd just picture in his mind how fine it was going to look when he was through."

"I do that with cooking, kind of. I see all the ingredients out there and picture what it's going to look like."

She slapped her knee. "I like that!"

But when it came to thinking about the mess of my education, I couldn't get a picture in my mind about how it would look if I could clean it up. I had no idea where to start.

"Let me tell you a secret, Foster. When you've got a

big problem, just start somewhere. Do one little thing to make it better. Then do another little thing, and another."

"Is that why you keep tending the garden?"

"That's right. Bit by bit, I'm doing something. I'm going to be planting tulip bulbs and daffodils in the fall to get ready for spring."

I tried to picture this church open and surrounded by flowers, but I couldn't quite do it. I smiled at her. "I think Perseverance is the perfect name for you."

She laughed. "It's my middle name. I hated it when I was young, but over the years, it's just moved to the front of my life."

I took a deep breath. "My middle name's Akilah. It means 'intelligent one who reasons.'"

"You grab hold of that," Perseverance told me. "That name's a gift your parents gave you."

I looked down. "I don't feel like I deserve it."

"That's okay, honey," she said. "You don't have to right now. But bit by bit, start cleaning up whatever's in your way." She stood up and grabbed her hoe. "I've got work to do."

I smiled. "Yes ma'am, you sure do."

Twenty-Seven

"TRIPLE CHOCOLATE CUPCAKES," I announced to Angry Wayne. "Two dozen."

He was out front cleaning off two round tables and chairs. He'd never had outdoor seating. "Think you can bring three dozen?" he asked me.

"I don't know."

"Because I had a woman who'd driven over from Harrington to buy some of your cupcakes, and we were sold out."

That was nice to hear. "I don't think I could deliver three dozen myself, sir. I'd need help."

He nodded and looked at the dirty front window. "You think I should get curtains?"

I was having trouble picturing that. Jim Bob the tarantula crawled under the round tables. This seemed like a good time to head to Miss Charleena's.

★ ★ ★

I laid out the Elvis book on Miss Charleena's counter and read the first sentence and half of the next one about how Elvis's mother was buried at Graceland, which made me wonder where Lester's daddy was buried. I wondered if it was out by the tomato patch where Lester spent so much time. The tomatoes were ripe now.

"I'd say you've had a serious breakthrough, Foster McFee."

I pushed her pretty blue paper toward her and said, "Write down for me what you just said."

Miss Charleena did. *I'd say you've had a serious breakthrough, Foster McFee.*

"Put the date on it," I told her.

July 31st.

"You want me to sign it?"

"Yes, ma'am."

Charleena Hendley.

She put a squiggle line under her name. I bet this was worth some money, but I'd never sell it, not ever.

Miss Charleena was wearing a pretty white shirt with lace around the neck. It looked like the top of my white dress I wore for the sixth-grade moving up ceremony. That dress got ruined with one of the worst words in the English language—LIMITED.

Why was I thinking about that? I'd just had an official signed and dated breakthrough.

"What's the matter, Foster?"

"Nothing."

I looked at the blue paper she'd signed. I tried to read what she'd written and got all messed up. The words were a jumble to me.

"Foster, what's wrong?"

"I've got to go," I told her.

"No." She put her hands on my shoulders and sat me down. "Not this time. You tell me what just happened."

"Your shirt reminded me of something I used to have."

"What was that?"

"A white dress."

Miss Charleena touched the lace around her neck.

"It was an important dress. And it got ruined. I don't mean I spilled on it; it got ruined in another way. In sixth grade."

"Do you still have it?"

"My mama kept it. She said it was historic."

"Does it still fit?"

"I guess so."

"Bring it over," she said.

"You mean here?"

"I mean here."

* * *

I got the box with the white dress out of the storage bin under the couch, and put the box on the table as Lester's daddy's stupid, dead fish looked on. After that awful moving-up ceremony, Mama told me how proud she was and how pretty I looked. She had the dress dry-cleaned, put it in the box, and covered it with pink paper. Opening this box was like upsetting a hornet's nest. All the bad feelings swarmed around.

LIMITED

limited

limited

I thought of speed limit signs. I always went slower in school, like I was crawling.

I took the pink paper off and lifted the dress up. For a minute I remembered when Mama and I had found it at the Second Chance Store. Mama held it up, grinning.

I didn't see what was so great. It looked old-fashioned

to me, but Mama sees things others can't see, like Perseverance Wilson.

"I'll cut you a pretty new neckline, put some lace going up to your neck, give this a tuck around your waist. You'll be a real heartbreaker."

What she didn't know was my heart was the one that would be breaking.

She sewed up a storm and made that dress into something so special. I never told her about how I felt wearing it. I didn't want to hurt her feelings.

"I haven't seen that dress for the longest time." It was Mama. She walked over and held it up. "I remember you coming down the aisle in this."

Me too.

She flopped in the lean-back chair and kicked her shoes off. "I'm not leaving this chair," she said. Her phone started ringing.

Mama groaned. "Get it, Baby."

I fished it out of her purse. "Hello," I said. "This is Foster speaking."

"Well, now, my Foster child, I sure miss seeing you."

I felt the hair crawl on my neck.

"How do you like living in West Virginia, girl?

Guess what? I've got a cousin near Culpepper."

I turned to Mama, but she was sleeping.

"My cousin, he plays guitar. I'm coming up to see him, and, of course, I'll be paying a special visit to you and that mama of yours."

"We're not in Culpepper anymore," I said. I hoped my voice didn't sound as scared as I felt. "We moved yesterday."

Mama sat straight up.

"Your mama didn't tell me that!"

"She got a new job," I lied. "A real good new job."

"Doing what?"

"Singing."

"Who is it, Baby?"

Lies were pouring out of me. "And she's got a new boyfriend, too, who's just like my daddy."

"I don't like what you're telling me, girl!"

Ask me if I care.

I pressed the red button. No more Huck. I stood there shaking.

Mama walked toward me. "What are you doing?"

"I'm protecting us." The phone started ringing. Mama headed for it. "Don't answer it, Mama!"

"I'm not." She turned the phone off.

"I want to know what happened to your arm," I told her.

"Foster, I've had a long day at work."

"I want to know what's going on!"

Mama stood there holding the phone. The light through the little round window shone around her hair. She looked soft and gentle like an angel.

"All right. I'll tell you."

Twenty-Eight

"I NEED TO let you know what it was like for me when I was growing up," Mama began. "My daddy was a hard man, and sometimes," she took a huge breath, "he hit my mother."

I sat perfectly still.

"And she got used to it, I guess. Once she called the police on him, but his cousin was on the force and he covered the whole thing up. I'm not using this as an excuse, but it's what I know."

"Did grandpa ever hurt you?"

"No. But knowing he hurt Mama hurt me. I'd go to my friends' houses and see their papas who weren't like mine. I wanted to live in another family. I wanted to run away, and eventually I did." She smiled sadly. "Now, I was careful to avoid men like my daddy. When I met your father, he was the gentlest, sweetest man. But he was strong, too, and what a combination. Lord, I miss that man." She sat there in the chair, eyes closed.

I waited for a minute, then I had to ask. "How come you ended up with Huck?"

She shook her head sadly. "Oh, Huck. I wish I could turn back the clock on that. I just wanted to sing and he kept promising me he'd help me. I can tell you, Foster, and this is God's honest truth. That night Huck broke the window and came into the apartment was the only time he hurt me. Something in me just snapped. I had to get us out of there fast."

"You did that."

Mama rubbed her forehead with her fingers. "And when I knew we'd left your daddy's pillowcase behind and Huck had it, I had to get it for you. That's the only reason I went back."

I believed her.

"I only saw him for an hour, and when I was heading out the door, he grabbed my arm and yanked it so hard, but I left anyway. That's how I got the bruise." She looked down. "I didn't fall."

"I didn't think you did."

She took my hand. Her fingers were strong. "I'm sorry I lied to you, Foster. I haven't told many people about my growing up."

I gave her a big hug. She had tears in her eyes. "Mama, he knows we're in Culpepper."

"I heard that."

"That's not good."

"No, it isn't."

"Do you think he believed me when I said we'd moved?"

She smiled. "I hope so."

"Did you like the part when I said you had a new boyfriend like daddy?"

"That was definitely my favorite part."

★ ★ ★

I started picturing Huck behind every bush. I told Macon, Garland, and Amy to be on the lookout for a yellow Cadillac that honked out "Jailhouse Rock."

I didn't feel safe. When I saw the two prisoners from the work release program cleaning up the street, I ran away fast. When I worked at Helping Hands, I kept wondering if Huck was going to burst in and do something awful. This new lady, Val, had just come to stay for a few days with her little daughter, Pearly, and her baby boy named Babcock.

"You ever been real afraid of somebody you know real well?" Val asked me.

"Yes," I told her. "I know what that's like."

She gave Babcock a bottle. "I came here to tell my husband, Duke, we can't be together anymore. I want a divorce. He's not going to like it."

At least Duke was in jail and couldn't get out. I thought about Huck out there looking for us. Pearly skipped into the kitchen with a picture she'd colored. "You give this to Daddy," she told Val.

I opened my Bake and Take. I had vanilla cupcakes with sprinkles. "You want one?"

Pearly's eyes got big. Val smiled. "I used to make cupcakes with my grandma when I was a girl. I think that was the sweetest time of my life."

* * *

It wasn't too sweet at the Church of God FOR SALE. Taco Terrific was buying the property. Perseverance Wilson tried to get Mr. Fish to change his mind, but he wouldn't. The contract was going through.

More people started wearing taco T-shirts with Xs

through them. All of this was hard on Amy.

"I told Daddy he shouldn't sell the church, but he's scared about money. He's always been that way."

"It's not your fault," I told her.

Amy shook her head. "I walk down the street and feel like people can't stand us."

"They can't stand your father," Macon said. "Not you."

I elbowed him.

The weather was hot, and Lester's tomatoes were fat, red, and juicy. I made bruschetta, which is grilled bread with olive oil, garlic, and tomatoes. Lester ate so much of it he had to lie down.

And the funniest thing happened with my reading. I started telling people I was working hard at it—and instead of laughing, they said, "How can we help?"

Garland told me the reason he was jumping fences was to build up his leg muscles. "You're just building up your brain muscles, Foster."

Val at Helping Hands helped me read a little book to Pearly about a puppy that got lost and found its way home. Macon made word cards for me so I could practice. Mama and I created an alphabet food game.

"A is for . . ."

"Aioli," I said. That's a sauce.

She grinned. "B is for . . ."

"Butter."

"C is for . . ."

"*Cupcake!*"

Going further down the alphabet, *U* is for *under-cooked*.

I created a chocolate cupcake with peanut-butter frosting. I gave Mama the first bite and she said, "Take these out of this house or I'll eat every last one. Run!" I brought them to Angry Wayne's and they sold out fast. Muffins are good, don't get me wrong, but sometimes a cupcake just has your name on it.

Miss Charleena said her problem was that every cupcake had her name on it.

"I'm still waiting to see that dress of yours," she reminded me.

Twenty-Nine

I SLAPPED THE box with the white dress in it on Miss Charleena's counter.

"Let's see," she directed.

I opened the box, took off the pink paper, and lifted the dress up.

"That's beautiful, Foster."

"Yes ma'am."

"And how did it get ruined?"

I lowered it and told her. "It was the dress I wore for the moving-up ceremony at my old school. I got out of that school by the skin of my teeth—that's what my one teacher said."

"And that dress carries that memory for you."

I told her about being limited.

"That's an ugly word. You're not at that school anymore."

"I know." The problem was the dress didn't know it.

"I just want to put it back for right now, Miss Charleena."

"I've got a box, too." She put a bendy straw in her chocolate milk and headed down the hall. I followed. She stopped at a closet and opened the doors. It was so big, you could walk in. She dragged a step stool over, stepped on it, and reached for a little box on the top shelf.

She stepped down and handed the box to me.

"What's in it?"

"Something awful."

The box didn't look big enough to have anything inside that was too awful. She walked into the living room and sat on her white couch. I sat down, too.

"Open it," she said.

I did, and there was an envelope. I handed it to her. Her face got very stern as she took out the papers in the envelope and read, "Mike Tuller finds Bliss."

"What does that mean?"

"Mike Tuller was my husband, and he started seeing a supermodel while we were married. Her name was Bliss. It was in all the magazines. I was devastated, humiliated. They were parading all over the world, this happy, perfect couple."

"That's awful."

She held up a magazine. "'Charleena's Agony.' That was the headline. It sure sold magazines." She sat back. "The reporters wouldn't leave me alone. They waited outside my house and followed me, taking photographs. They talked to my friends, my family. They wanted to record every tear I shed, and there were lots of tears."

"I can't imagine how hard that was, Miss Charleena."

She smiled sadly and looked at her closed curtains.

"It's a pretty day out," I told her.

"I've missed a lot of pretty days, Foster. Back when I was acting, I was fairly well known—people recognized me in restaurants or driving down the street. But when my husband left me and it all went public, then I hit the big time. I was famous for being a jilted wife."

I didn't know what to say.

"Fame can look good from the outside, darlin', but it can be a mean game. It plays by its own rules." She closed the box.

"How did you get over it, Miss Charleena?"

"It took me a long time. I put some of the headlines from the magazines around the house. At first I could hardly stand the pain of looking at them and feeling betrayed. The photos of them so happy and me so miserable. But after a while, I got angry, and I thought, thank God I'm not married anymore to a man who would do a thing like that."

"Is that why you came here to live?"

"I needed to get away from Hollywood like you can't believe."

"Do you miss acting?"

She grinned. "Yes, I do. But Stan called today."

"Your agent?"

"The one and only. Stan still believes in me."

"Well, I believe in you, Miss Charleena. You're the greatest actor I've ever known. The only one I've ever known, but still."

"Stan sent me a script. It might be the best way for me to stick my foot back into acting." She laughed. "They want me to do the voice-over for a horse in a feature cartoon."

"That's cool."

She handed me a stack of papers with a cover. "That's the script. Read the first scene to me."

I'd never seen a script before. It looked different from a book. To begin with, there weren't nearly as many words on the page. I liked that. I'm not sure what she meant by the first scene. The first words didn't make sense.

Fade in:

"I don't know what this means," I told her.

"Fade in. It means the movie is starting, the camera is coming to rest on what you need to see."

"Okay." Now that I could read how Elvis loved his mother, I was feeling brave. I took a deep breath. "Fade in," I read, "on a . . . black horse." I looked up. "Is that right?"

"Keep going."

"The horse . . . is . . ." I looked up again, pointed to the words.

"Running," she said.

"Across a plain?" I wasn't sure if that was right.

She nodded. "You've got my interest."

"Now . . . we see . . . another horse." I'm reading slow, but I'm reading! I look at her. "I like this script, it's got short sentences."

"Keep reading."

"This horse has a . . . a rider. The rider has a rope. Uh-oh . . . wait. The uh-oh isn't in the script."

"My favorite line's coming." She leaned forward.

I focused extra hard. "The horse and rider are . . ." This was so hard. ". . . trying to catch the black horse, but . . . wait, now I get it! But she is . . . faster. Then we hear the black horse say . . . um . . ." I looked at the script. Couldn't make out the words. "What does this mean?"

Miss Charleena threw back her head, made an excellent horse sound, and said, "'*Toodles, turkey.*'"

I laughed. "We hear the black horse say, 'Toodles, turkey!' And the black horse . . ." My brain was aching. "The black horse speeds away across the plain."

"Brilliant," she told me.

I felt like throwing that script up in the air!

"You know what's great about that scene?" Miss Charleena asked.

"It's exciting!"

"Yeah."

"It's funny what the black horse says."

"That's right, and with only two words, we know who that black horse is. She's fast and she's not going to take any guff from anything or anybody."

I looked down at the script, thinking, *Please don't ask me to read any more. I just want to be with all the words I got right.*

"You think I should take this part, Foster McFee?"

"Yes, ma'am. You'd be an awesome horse."

"Well, before I lose my nerve . . ." Miss Charleena grabbed the phone and punched in numbers. "Stan, are you sitting down . . . ? Well, sit down, Stanley, because I'm coming out of retirement." She was nodding and laughing her great earthy laugh. "Yes, I really mean it . . . yes, Stan, you can take it to the bank, but only ten percent of it."

I opened her curtains without asking, and light shone all over.

"Well, now," she said, laughing. "What else should I let into my life?"

Thirty

MISS CHARLEENA WROTE a check to Helping Hands and asked me to take it over. I walked into the kitchen, and Val was talking to another one of the wives.

"I told Duke I'm leaving him, and he didn't like that." Her hands were shaking.

"You have to do what's right for you," the other wife said.

"Duke scares me," Val said. "He's always scared me. They've got him out on this work release, and he's got everybody fooled that he's changed. I know he hasn't!"

I think *I've* got problems.

I found Perseverance Wilson and gave her the pretty blue envelope with Miss Charleena's check. She ripped that thing open and shouted, "Hallelujah!" Then she started making plans. "We're going to put a fresh coat of paint in all the rooms, we're going to get pretty curtains on those windows, fix the staircase, and—"

"My mama's good at windows," I told her. "She says a pretty window makes the rest of the world look friendly, even if it's not."

"Call your mama, honey. We're turning this old place around."

★ ★ ★

There was a meeting that night of people who wanted to help. Garland was there and Macon, Mama, me, and Amy. Part of my job was keeping the little kids at Helping Hands out of everyone's hair. I brought my baking pans—because, really, what kid doesn't like to bake?

Macon had just got his first camera phone, and he was a dangerous person. I scratched my neck and he filmed me. I walked out of the bathroom and he filmed me. He caught Amy picking her nose. Garland didn't do gross things in public, so he didn't get filmed much.

I was in the Helping Hands kitchen with the kids, making up the batter for Sonny's Bake 'Em Proud Cupcakes. I wondered how he was doing.

"You're all cooks in training," I told them. Baby Babcock threw some measuring spoons at his sister.

"Stop it!" Pearly screamed.

I gave him back the spoons and showed him how to shake them like a rattle. Babcock shook those spoons with everything he had.

"Cupcakes are everywhere today," I told the kids. "And you can decorate each one with different colored frosting."

"I want blue frosting," Pearly said.

Amy sat down. "I want purple frosting with orange sprinkles, a cherry on top, and sparklers."

"Sparklers!" the kids said.

I glared at Amy. "No sparklers."

Mama was measuring the kitchen windows as Babcock shook the spoons in a kind of rhythm. Her foot started tapping out the beat, then she pointed a finger at Babcock and sang out:

Come on, babe, you've got to shake that thing!
You've got to shake it in the morning.

Babcock shook it.

You've got to shake it in the night.
You've got to shake it, shake it, shake it,
Now it's going to be all right! Wooooooo!

Babcock raised his little arms, and she sang it again loud and strong as people came into the kitchen.

Percy said, "Where have you been hiding that voice?"

Mama smiled. "I just had it packed away."

"Sing something else, Mrs. McFee." Pearly had chocolate batter on her forehead and in her hair.

Val walked into the kitchen and said, "Yes, sing."

"Well . . . here's a little lullaby I used to sing to Foster."

I laughed.

Mama stood there for a minute, then her right foot started tapping, her right hand began to slap her thigh in a different rhythm. She was moving her shoulders to the beat.

Mmmmmm, little one. Close your eyes for the day is done. Oh, oh, oh . . .
You're going to sleep so sweet because God is watching over you.

She clapped. "Sing it out!"

Mmmmmm, little one. Close your eyes for the day is done . . .

Mama cranked up the volume.

Sleep sweet for you are never, no never alone!

Everyone applauded.

"Could you get to sleep after your mom sang that to you?" Pearly asked me.

"No way!"

Perseverance Wilson stepped forward. "One thing I know after that song. You need to give a real concert."

* * *

Baking with children isn't for weak people. I am definitely going to mention this when I get on the Food Network. I put the pans in the oven. "These are going to be so good!"

That's when the front door opened. A man in a gray uniform with angry eyes burst in saying, "I don't want any trouble. I'm just here to get my family."

Pearly dropped the wooden spoon on the floor and whispered, "Daddy."

Thirty-One

"HI THERE, HONEY," the man said. "Where's Mommy?"

Pearly started crying.

"I asked you a question!"

I looked at Macon, who didn't move. Babcock was crawling on the floor.

"What are you doing here, Duke?" Val was standing in the door now. "You're not supposed to be out yet."

"Looks like I'm out, don't it?"

"We're not going with you, Duke. *I told you.*"

"Yes, you are." He walked over to her.

"I said we're not going!"

He reached for her arm, and Garland stepped between them. Mama came alongside Garland, followed by Perseverance Wilson, who said, "We don't want any trouble here." They formed a wall around Val.

"You'd best be leaving," Perseverance told him.

Duke headed to Pearly, who shouted, "No, Daddy!"

Mama rushed to Pearly. "That's enough, Duke! You're way out of bounds."

"I've got a knife. Don't make me use it."

Babcock started crying.

Not now, Babcock! I scooped him up. Mama took Pearly by the hand. "It's okay." She led her to Val as the oven timer buzzed.

"What's that?" Duke shouted.

I gulped. "Cupcakes."

"Cupcakes?"

"Vanilla and chocolate."

I handed Babcock to Amy. "I need to get them out of the oven, and then me and the kids are going to make frosting."

Duke just stood there.

"I'm going to take them out now," I told him. I put on my oven mitt and walked to the stove with more courage than I felt. "You ever bake, sir?"

"No."

"The thing you look for in cupcakes is if they're springy when you touch them. That means they're done."

I opened the door, and I swear to you, if I could have, I would have crawled inside. I touched the cupcakes. They sprung back. He was standing there watching. "They're done." I took the pan out.

"I'm going to let them cool on this rack. Don't they look good? You're not going to believe the secret ingredient."

Duke was staring at them. I glanced at Garland, who looked like he was ready to defend the world.

"Okay, now, I'm going to start making the frosting. Is that all right?"

Duke nodded.

Perseverance Wilson said, "How did you get here, Duke?"

"I got here."

"Did they let you out of the prison?"

He laughed. "I let myself out."

On the Food Network they have these shows where chefs have to cook with strange ingredients while the clock is ticking. But I bet there's never once been a show where you have to do this in the kitchen with an escaped convict.

My hands were shaking as I put the butter in the bowl and plugged in the hand mixer. I'm thinking if

Duke gets too close to me I'll shove the mixer in his face.

Pearly cried out. "I want to help. You said I could help!"

Val burst through the line of women. "Get out of here, Duke! You always ruin everything!"

He headed toward her, but Garland stood tough.

Macon was typing something on his phone. Then he held it out where Duke couldn't see and started filming.

I took a big breath. "Okay," I said, "in case you've never made frosting before, here's what you've got to know. See how this butter is good and creamy? That's the secret to good frosting. Now I'm going to add the confectioners' sugar and beat it until it's fluffy." I did that and Mama brought over Pearly, who was shaking and crying.

"I haven't had a cupcake in a long time," Duke said.

"I made cupcakes," Val insisted.

"Shut up."

Perseverance Wilson and Garland came behind Duke like they were going to jump him, but he turned around and grabbed Babcock from Amy's arms. "Don't try anything funny."

Val screamed, "You give him to me!"

Babcock was crying and reaching for his mother. A

shout rose up in my throat, but that's where it stayed. Duke shook his head and said, "We're just having a good time here, aren't we, little guy?"

"Dada."

That got to Duke. "That's right," he whispered. "I'm your dada."

I didn't think my heart could beat this hard and stay in my chest. "Okay, I'm beating the vanilla in." Mama lifted Pearly up so she could see. "I'm adding chopped chocolate and beating it until it's shiny. Watch this."

I beat it for another two minutes, which seems like four days when an escaped convict is watching you.

I put the frosting in the bowl on the table and got another bowl. "I'm going to make vanilla frosting now, and we're going to color some of it blue."

"I know who that's for," Duke said, smiling at Pearly.

I made the vanilla frosting fast, put some in a cup, and got out the blue food coloring. "We only need a drop. There. You mix it up."

Pearly grinned and stirred it.

"It's pretty." She tasted it. "Taste it, Daddy."

Duke tasted it. "You know what day it is?"

"Tuesday," Amy said.

"It's my birthday." Duke said it like the saddest man who ever walked.

Pearly took a cupcake and put blue frosting on it and sprinkles. "Happy birthday, Daddy."

"You not going to sing to me?" he asked her.

Pearly's little lip was shaking as she began, "Happy birthday to you . . ." She couldn't keep it up. But then Mama sang out a happy birthday that shook the walls.

"I heard you on the radio," Duke said.

"Not yet," Mama told him.

Macon motioned to the window with his eyes. Angry Wayne was outside. He winked at me and then he was gone.

Duke ate the cupcake, and Babcock watched him. He ate four more with M&M's on top.

"I'm going now," he said.

"We're not going with you," Val told him.

"I'm going alone." He handed Babcock to Val. "I'm sorry. I'm real sorry." He ran out the back door. Pearly ran up the stairs crying.

"I got all of it," Macon whispered, and put his phone down.

I heard a noise outside, sounds of a fight, then shouting. *"I'm making a citizen's arrest!"*

We all ran out. Wayne had Duke on the ground, and Garland ran over to help hold him down. Amy ran over, too. We heard a siren.

The sheriff's car roared up. He put Duke in handcuffs and led him away. Duke looked back at us sadly as Val started crying.

Barry and Larry ran over. "Awesome, Pop. Awesome!"

Angry Wayne brushed himself off and put his hand on each of their shoulders. "A man's gotta do what a man's gotta do."

Thirty-Two

"YOU DON'T KNOW the power of a cupcake until your life depends on it."

I said this to a reporter from the *West Virginia Star*. She looked at me like I was crazy, but plenty of people in town understood.

I'm not sure things would have gone so well if I'd been making muffins when Duke showed up. I'm not saying muffins, cookies, and pies don't have their place. But there's something about a cupcake that gets inside of people and helps them be the best they can be. I'd found my voice in the baking world.

My cupcakes were now officially famous in Culpepper. Angry Wayne put a blackboard sign out front of his restaurant:

PREPARE TO MEET YOUR BAKER

People were sitting outside eating cupcakes, griping about the world.

"We're getting a sight too fancy 'round here," Clay complained as Mama hung the plaid curtains she'd made in Wayne's window.

I had a new Bake and Take that carried thirty-six cupcakes. I made them big and proud, and Angry Wayne sold every one as I stood by the counter and people came up to say hey.

"Child's gifted," Clay said.

"Heard you saved the day," Betty added.

I shook my head. "We all worked together."

All of Culpepper was celebrating, except for Pearly and Val. Pearly was so quiet as they got into their car to leave. Babcock was in his car seat shaking his spoons.

"I've got a present for you," I told Pearly. "A special baker's present. I'm going to name a cupcake after you."

"*You are?*"

"Pearly's True Blue Cupcakes."

"True blue," she said.

"You are definitely that." I hugged her hard.

Val got in the car and drove off.

* ★ *

Miss Charleena was practicing her neigh. She was leaving for Hollywood soon, and I was scared she wouldn't come back.

"You don't have to worry about that. I'll always come back home."

"It's going to be more exciting where you're going."

"Yes, but I belong here."

I understood that. I belong here, too. Knowing you belong is like putting frosting on a cupcake. It totally seals the deal.

"I learned something about your new school, Foster."

I tried to look positive.

"I called over there and told them about how we've been working together. . . ."

"You turned me in?"

"I talked to the principal."

"She hates me!"

"Sorry, to burst your bubble, darlin'. But after the way you handled yourself with Duke, she respects you."

"It won't last."

"My, you're a joy to be with today."

I sat there.

"She said they have a reading teacher, Mrs. Vick, who specializes in what you need. She's coming to your mama's concert, and you can meet her."

Mama was giving a concert to support Helping Hands.

"I don't want to meet her at the concert." I took chocolate cherry brownies out of the oven. "I want you to keep teaching me."

Miss Charleena folded her arms, "Foster, I'm not a teacher and I'm sure not a specialist in reading. I've taken you as far as I know. It's time for the A team to come in. But you've made wonderful progress over the summer." She handed me a piece of her pretty blue paper with the words, *The honor of your presence is requested at the graduation of Miss Foster McFee of Culpepper, West Virginia. Foster will be receiving her reading diploma with honors.*

I couldn't read it all, so Miss Charleena had to help me, but once I got the concept, you could have knocked me over.

"I didn't know there'd be a graduation."

"Oh, yes."

"I didn't know there'd be a diploma!"

She nodded.

"And . . ." I could hardly say it. "With *honors*?" I had to double-check.

She grinned. "Make sure to wear your white dress."

⋆ ⋆ ⋆

I was standing in Miss Charleena's hall in my white dress. I never thought I'd wear it again. People were seated in the living room—Mama, Macon, Kitty, Lester, Amy, Garland, and Perseverance Wilson. Miss Charleena, who was dressed in a blue suit with her hair pulled back, made her big entrance and said in her acting voice, "Ladies and gentlemen, we are here to celebrate a remarkable achievement."

That was my cue to come out and walk over to her, but I couldn't come out right away because I was crying. Miss Charleena walked back to the hall where I was and didn't say a thing about my tears because she was crying a little, too.

"You ready?" she asked me.

"Yes, ma'am."

"I am so proud to know you, darlin'."

We walked out together, student and teacher, although close to everybody in that room had been my teacher.

Mama was crying, and Kitty was grinning. Lester

shouted, "All right, all right!" Macon stood on a chair for his own reasons and clapped till his face turned red. Garland and Amy did the wave.

Miss Charleena handed me a diploma for reading. "Foster Akilah McFee, you have graduated with honors in reading achievement over the summer. The sky is the limit for you now."

And with those words she wiped LIMITED off my mind and heart forever.

"Speech, speech," Macon cried, but I didn't want to make a speech. I just stood there as the bad memories flew away.

* * *

I put my diploma on the bed, opened the Las Vegas pillowcase, and took out Daddy's letters. I tried to see his face, but I couldn't quite do it. I tried to hear his voice, but it was a faraway memory. I opened the thickest envelope. It was a birthday letter Daddy had sent me. I unfolded the letter, smoothed it out on the bed.

"Dear Foster," I said out loud. It's much easier to read a book than someone's printing, but slowly I saw the pattern. I couldn't get all of it, but that didn't matter.

How are you? I hope it's colder where you are. Right now
the temperature here is so hot we have to drink extra
water. I wish I could have been home for your birthday.
I remember when you were little and you would bake
with that little oven. You'd sing happy birthday to yourself
even when it wasn't your birthday. You always understood
about celebrating.

Today in this faraway place, I'm thinking about you
and your mom and missing you both very much. I'm
so proud of you both. I think some of the guys here are
jealous that I've got such a good family. So you stay strong
and know that on the other side of the world is a guy who
loves you like crazy!

See you soon, Baby.

Love, Dad

I picked out enough of it to get the concept. I was
probably the most loved kid in the world.

Thirty-Three

"I NEED TO tell you something." Macon and I were walking back from FOOD. "You know the movies I took of Duke and of your mama singing?"

"Yeah."

"I feel so stupid. They didn't come out. All I got was a couple of knees, and everything was fuzzy. I forgot to turn the sound on."

"It was a pretty crazy time," I reminded him.

"But that could have been my big breakthrough as a director!"

"I've had plenty of cakes that didn't turn out."

"I need to practice more," he groaned.

A yellow car pulled up.

My heart stopped.

I dropped the bag of groceries as Huck jumped out dressed like Elvis.

My mouth got dry as he swaggered over. "Now, you don't look happy to see me."

I took a step back.

"I'm happy to see you, girl. You've always been my Foster child."

"I'm not your Foster child!"

"Don't go getting huffy."

And right then, all the fears of Elvis I'd had, all the dreams about getting carried back to Memphis, all the nightmares of Huck hurting us, didn't matter. I'd baked cupcakes for an escaped convict and lived to tell about it. I wasn't going to let an Elvis impersonator scare me.

"I've come to see your mama," he said.

"She doesn't want to see you."

He smoothed his sideburns. "I know that's not true."

"That's your problem," I told him.

"You're acting downright hostile to me, girl."

"Glad you noticed, Huck."

"I think," Macon said, "that she doesn't want you bothering her anymore."

Huck looked at Macon like a snake looks at a mouse. "Little boy, don't you talk to me like that!"

Macon took out his camera phone and held it up. "I'm Macon Dillard. I make documentary films."

"Turn on the volume," I whispered, and Macon did.

Huck stepped forward. "You listen to the King!"

"You're not the king here or anywhere," I told him. "Get away from me and get away from my mama!"

He didn't budge, but I didn't either.

"Put that thing down," he said to Macon.

"No, sir."

"I said put that down!"

"Get away from us!" I shouted. "And get away from my mama!" I shouted it again. "You hear me, Huck? *Get away from us and get away from my mama!*"

I kept shouting it. Macon joined in, too, while holding up his camera.

And that's when the sheriff drove up. He got out of the car like sheriffs do in the movies. "What's going on here?"

Huck looked real nervous.

"You bothering these kids?"

"Yes!" Macon and I shouted together.

"Let me see some ID, sir."

Huck fumbled in his wallet. "I know the girl and her mama, and I just came to pay them a call." He handed his license over.

The sheriff looked at the old yellow Cadillac with

his Elvis decal and the notes going over the hood. "That your car?"

Huck nodded.

"Well, to begin with your license is expired. Let's see what else we can find." The sheriff looked at me and Macon. "You be on your way now. I got this under control."

★ ★ ★

We went to Fish Hardware and showed Mama Macon's movie. It was tilted and it jumped around a lot, but you could still get the idea. Then on her lunch break, Mama went over to the emergency care office where the nurse took the photo of her bruised eye when we first got to town.

"I want to press charges against the man who hit me," Mama told the nurse. "How do I do that?"

The nurse called the sheriff's office. "They've got him in custody, Mrs. McFee."

There was something strong in Mama now. What was inside of her was coming out for all the world to see.

★ ★ ★

"Tonight we're going to celebrate an organization whose sole purpose is helping people." Miss Charleena said this, standing on a little stage.

All the people of Culpepper applauded.

Miss Charleena smiled at Mama, who was smoothing down her sparkly top. "And to help us do that, I am delighted to welcome one of our own to this stage. Put on your seat belts, folks, and let's hear it for Rayka McFee!"

Rocking music started playing as Mama walked to the mic looking gorgeous. I was sitting with Garland, Macon, and Amy, moving to the beat. Mama sang low and strong.

Left a good job down in the city
Working for the man every night and day.

She was wailing; people were nodding.

"Sing it," Angry Wayne shouted.

Sing it, Mama. Sing it *out*.

And she did about the big wheels that keep on turning. I looked over at Amy, whose mouth hung open. Garland said to me, "Your mama rocks."

Oh yeah.

It was like she was made for a stage, the way she stood there and sang. She sang show tunes, she sang blues.

"*Summertime,*" she sang out low and full, "*and the living is easy.*"

I closed my eyes. Mama was singing from the part of her that had been held back for so long. I knew where the power in her voice came from—all the times she didn't give up, all the times she sang backup and let somebody else be the star, all the times she belted out songs in the shower and in the car. It came from that long year when she had nodules on her throat and she couldn't sing. It came from loving and losing Daddy. It came from loving me.

She sang "Foster's Song" pure and clear like a bird.

Hush now, it's gonna be all right.
The night is coming, but we've got the light . . .

Amy leaned forward. "I want to learn that."

Song after song—she brought us up stomping and clapping and down to a place where everyone could feel the hurt. And she was up again . . .

I watched her, and as I did I knew she couldn't go back to just singing backup after this. Mama closed her eyes and sang a song she'd written not long after Daddy died. She hadn't sung it for close to forever.

There is nothing like a song.
It flies into your heart and stays all day long . . .

She sang it low, she sang it high. And people started singing it with her. Amy's voice rang out so pretty. I grinned at her. "You're good!"

Flowers were swaying in the wind like they had a song inside them. Mama's voice touches every living thing.

She got a standing ovation at the end. It didn't seem like people were ever going to stop applauding, but after a while, they did.

My part was coming up. It was time to eat.

I could have brought more cupcakes. There was a long line waiting to buy food.

"Step up, folks," Garland said. "We've got all of Foster's specialties in one place. Any kind of cupcake you've ever dreamed of, butterscotch muffins, cherry brownies. It doesn't get any better than this!"

"You can come on by any morning and have these at my restaurant," Angry Wayne shouted.

It was the ultimate bake sale. Jim Bob the tarantula crawled under the food table. Only a few people screamed. People were eating, smiling, getting crumbs on each other, and laughing.

Everyone was saying, "Your mama should make a record, your mama's the best singer we've ever heard." Mama was surrounded by people. She was talking to a man who gave her a business card. They talked some more and Mama was nodding and smiling and the man was, too.

Then a gray cloud showed up. "Well, my dear, you must be awfully proud of your mother." It was Mrs. Dupree, the principal, and she had another lady with her.

I looked down. "I'm real proud."

"I wanted to introduce you to Mrs. Vick. She's our reading specialist."

Garland cleared his throat. Macon elbowed me. I said, "Nice to meet you, ma'am."

She was eating one of my red velvet cupcakes. "I have never had a cupcake like this, and that's saying something. My family is in the restaurant business."

"You're kidding."

"I grew up in the kitchen," Mrs. Vick said happily.

"You know how to run a restaurant?"

"I do."

I wasn't sure this was the right thing to say. "Then how come you're not doing it?"

"I run one in the summer for my family on Mackinaw Island. I just got back."

Clay walked by, burping. "Child's gifted."

"I can see that." Mrs. Vick finished the cupcake.

★ ★ ★

I had a feeling cupcakes were going to play a big role in my education. I might do an entire show on how to impress a new teacher. Kids need to know the survival tools that are at their fingertips.

Macon stood next to me. "I need to ask you a question, and I want you to be honest."

"What?"

He looked down. "I want to know if you like Garland."

I tried not to blush. "He's . . . nice."

"Lots of people are nice, Foster. You know what I mean."

I stood there.

Macon looked up at me. "Do I have to spell this out?"

"I'm not that great at spelling."

He sputtered. "Are you, you know, *in like* with him?"

"In like?"

"Don't be difficult."

I looked over at Garland, who was grinning at me. I looked down, smiling, too.

"I knew it!" Macon said.

"I like him, Macon, but you're my best friend."

He thought about that. "You swear?"

"I swear. You don't have to worry."

"I was never worried, Foster!"

Betty walked up holding a vanilla cupcake in each hand. "Where in the world did you learn how to bake like this?"

I told her about Sonny's show and how he was in a hospital now, hurt bad. And as good as this day had been, a place of sadness opened up in me.

"I would imagine a letter from you could be just what the doctor ordered," Betty said.

I nodded and looked down.

"We could write the letter together," Macon said. "I could film you cooking. We could send that to Sonny!"

Thirty-Four

WE COULDN'T GET the letter right, because Macon kept wanting to say things that didn't sound like me. He was getting pretty bossy since he got his camera phone. Miss Charleena said that some directors get a big head, and I'd better get used to it.

I decided to give Sonny what I do best.

"Today on *Cooking with Foster*, we're going to make pineapple upside-down cupcakes with whipped cream. I created this recipe myself, and I'm dedicating it to Sonny Kroll, who taught me how to cook. I think it's going all the way to become an instant classic." I held up a pineapple slice and stood there.

Macon yelled, "Cut!"

"I was just going to cut it."

He sighed like I was stupid, but I didn't take that personally. I knew I was smart. "'Cut!' is what directors shout, Foster, when they want the action to stop. Tell us what you're doing and why you have the pineapple."

It's hard to do this in front of a real camera. "I'll try."

"Okay, roll it!" Macon shouted.

"I'm not making rolls, I'm making cupcakes."

"*Cut!*"

This wasn't working too well. Cooks on the Food Network have to put up with a lot.

"Take three," Macon shouted. I knew what that meant. It was the third time we were trying to get it right. I was getting sick of this. But then Macon smiled at me. "Just be yourself, Foster. That's the best thing in the world."

I started again, explained what I was doing with the pineapple. By mistake I dropped the pineapple on the floor. Macon's face got red, but I kept going.

"If no one's looking you can pretend like that didn't happen." I scooped up the pineapple and cut it up. I mentioned how you had to grease the cupcake pans extra well and not use paper liners. "We've got to turn the pan over at the end, and the cupcake comes out upside-down with the pineapple at the top."

I put butter, brown sugar, and pineapple in the bottom of each cupcake tin and filled it with batter.

"Now, we're going to pray this works," I said. "If you're just learning to bake, don't start with this recipe. This is for experts. I'd say the level of difficulty on this is hard. But you can't just be doing easy things in life. That's not what makes you smarter."

I put the pan in the oven. "But it's okay if you mess up. The most important thing about baking is to relax and be yourself. So don't go getting all perfect about everything, like if it doesn't look just like it does in the magazine, I can't cook it. You know, those magazines have tricks to make the food look good. But you and me—we don't need tricks. We're going to cook for people with all our hearts. That's the secret."

I started making the whipped cream. I'd put my beaters and bowl in the freezer—that makes the cream whip better. I turned the beaters on high. It's noisy, so it's hard to talk, but I screamed over the noise. "This is great because you can make it up early and put it in the refrigerator until you're ready!" I added a little confectioners' sugar to the whipped cream and tried it.

"Perfect!" I shouted. "And remember to turn off the beaters before you take them from the bowl. I forgot that once and got whipped cream all over myself.

These are just the lessons a baker learns in life."

The timer went off. I touched the tops of the cupcakes and they sprang back. "Okay, now here's where it can all go wrong. You put a knife along the sides of each cupcake to make sure it's loosened. You put a big plate over the pan and turn it over fast."

I did that and lifted the pan. All but two cupcakes came out with the pineapple sugar glaze on top. "I'd say that's a success!"

I got the whipped cream out, put a cupcake on a small plate. "Normally you let them cool before you put the whipped cream on, but sometimes you can't wait." I spooned the whipped cream on and took a bite. I closed my eyes like Sonny did and made a loud *mmmmmmmmm* sound.

"I want to tell you something I've learned. Cooking is about life. It gives us what we need to keep going, and it gives us something to share with other people. People don't think about that enough—so if you're a kid watching this, get out some pans and start practicing and see what food can do. And if you're an adult, don't stay stuck in the same old stuff you know, get out there with some fresh herbs and just go for it. And I don't want any letters about how you can't because your life is such and such a mess. I don't want to hear about that. I baked cupcakes once for an escaped convict, and they probably saved my life. I'm not making this up. I'll be telling you about that in the next show, but for now you just go for it and let your full self out. That's it until next time."

I waited for a minute as my heart pounded hard. "Feel better, Sonny! We're on this road together."

"Wave," Macon whispered.

I waved with my wooden spoon in my hand. I might use that move next time.

"Was that okay?" I asked him.

He lowered his camera. "More than okay."

* * *

Macon put the movie on the Internet, and we sent a letter to Sonny telling him it was there. Every day I wondered if I'd hear something. Mama was waiting, too. A man who had heard her sing wanted her to give a concert in Charleston.

Macon said you just have to keep going, no matter what, and he marched up to the Culpepper Prison and took his stand. He brought a stand, too. He put his camera phone on it, turned it on, and stood there seriously.

"I'm Macon Dillard and this is my town. It used to be different before this prison got built. There were promises made and broken and I've come to the Culpepper Prison to ask people *why*." He lowered his voice. "But no one will talk to me."

"Move it out of the way, kid," said the guard.

"See what I mean?" Macon said. "I know a prisoner behind these gray walls. His name is Duke."

"Thirty seconds, kid."

Macon glared at the guard. "I'm not giving up! I will get the truth and tell the people! I'll be back!"

The guard sneered. "Hey, whatever."

But he will be back, mister. You'll see.

"Don't give up," I told him.

"You either."

We headed home past the Church of God FOR SALE. Perseverance Wilson was taking down the FOR SALE sign, smiling. The church door was open.

I was glad to see she was dealing with the loss.

"They're not going to sell it," she said.

"You mean the church?"

Garland walked out. "The deal fell through."

"What happened?"

"Taco Terrific backed out." She clapped her hands and raised them high.

"Why?"

She looked up to heaven. "No one's quite sure, but we're just going to be thankful."

Thirty-Five

THE LETTER WAS on the kitchen counter when I got home. It had my name on it, and the other name in the upper left of the envelope said FOOD NETWORK. It looked just like it did on TV.

I held the envelope and then opened it so carefully. A photo of Sonny Kroll fell out; then I looked at the letter. My mind started to close up, and all the things that said I can't read came rushing back. They were sitting on my shoulder and whispering in my ear, *Don't even try.*

But I had a reading diploma with honors.

And, God knows, I had heart.

I sat down at the table, opened the letter, and unfolded it. It was from Sonny. At least I could tell someone had signed an S and then a squiggle

Dear Foster,

Thanks for your letter

I concentrated hard. My mind was not going to close up!

and thanks for your

I took the next words apart . . .

support during this tough time.

I tried to sound out *tough. Too? Tow?* It didn't make sense. I kept going.

The next sentence was long, but it mostly had easy words.

So you've been with me now for five years and you're not sick of me yet?

It took me some time to get that, but when I did, I laughed.

I'd say that's a fan.

But listen—about your cooking show. I saw it and I loved it. It really made my day.

I was grinning huge now. When I came to another long sentence, I just said each word slowly out loud.

I won't be doing my show for a while because I need to get better, but listen up—keep cooking. You're good. You hear me?

"I hear you."

Go out there and cook your heart out. Write me back, okay?

Sonny

I sat there holding the letter. *You don't know what you've given me, Sonny. You taught me to cook, and now you helped me read.*

I read it again. I read it out loud.

"Well now," Mama said. "Look what you're doing."

"I have to take it slow, but I can do it! You want to hear the letter, Mama?"

She sat down and nodded.

"How do you say t-o-u-g-h?"

"Tough."

I know about that!

I'll tell you something about tough things. They just about kill you, but if you decide to keep working at them, you'll find the way through. On the Food Network they have these shows where cooks have to put a meal together with all these weird ingredients. That's a lot like my life—dealing with things you wouldn't think could ever go together. But a good cook can make the best meal out of the craziest combinations.

When I get my own show, I'm going to talk about that.

But for now, I'm going to make the world a better place, one cupcake at a time.